A
HARLEQUIN
Book

PALACE OF THE PEACOCKS

by

VIOLET WINSPEAR

HARLEQUIN BOOKS
Winnipeg • Canada   New York • New York

PALACE OF THE PEACOCKS

This edition published in 1969 by Mills & Boon Limited,
50 Grafton Way, Fitzroy Square, London, England.

Harlequin Canadian edition published July, 1969
Harlequin U.S. edition published October, 1969

Standard Book Number: 373-51318-6.

CHAPTER ONE

The steamer was fully booked, the clerk told her. One of the more affluent passengers had cabin room to spare, but as he was a Mijnheer van Helden. . . .

The clerk shrugged and smiled in an ingratiating way, and Temple understood without words that had she been a man then Mijnheer van Helden could have been persuaded to share his cabin. 'I – I must get away on today's steamer,' she said distractedly. 'It will be a month before it returns to Lumbaya—'

The clerk spread his hands. There was nothing more he could do, and picking up her suitcase she turned away from the reception counter of the hotel, small, rather rundown, where she had been staying for the past month.

One month . . . twenty-eight days . . . such a short time in which to learn the pain of disillusion and the distress of having a dream shattered.

She went into the shabby lounge of the hotel, with dusty palms in tubs, and fans whirring lazily in the ceiling. She ordered a soft drink, and the shadows of the fans moved against the grubby white walls as she sat nursing a glass of iced pineapple juice. She sipped the juice and the ice rattled against the glass as a shiver ran through her. Inevitably her thoughts were on her meeting – the first after five years – with the man she had come all the way to Lumbaya to marry.

Even now she could hardly believe that Nick could change so drastically from the gay and charming young man she had known in England, who had been so full of ambition and promise.

'As soon as I'm made head office wallah,' he wrote to her, 'you can come out and we'll ring the wedding bells

5

together. The Company prefers its employees to be married and stable, and I know you'll love the tropics. Everything will appeal to that romantic imagination of yours ...'

Temple shivered in the sticky warmth of the hotel lounge. For five long years she had worked and saved and longed for the day when she would fly out to Nick and join him beneath the tropical sunshine and the flame trees ... all so colourful and different from Alford and the house in which she felt such an interloper.

She had stayed with Aunt Myra and her cousins so she could save that little bit extra each week. She had put up with her aunt's nagging and her cousins' airs and graces all for nothing.

For nothing!

That awful coldness crept through her again. She had to get away from Nick, but never in a hundred years would she return to Alford and that squabbling household where she had been the one who always helped with the chores, who made herself scarce when young men called for her cousins, who put up with being the orphan cousin who ought to feel grateful for a home. Life with Nick at Lumbaya had lain ahead of her and she had not complained.

Now her dream was ended. The Nick she had met in England – while sheltering from the rain in a bus shelter, of all places – had become a total stranger to her. One of those who had not been cast in the iron mould that life in the tropics demands of those who choose to work there.

The days are hot, the nights are exotic – and lonely for a man without a wife. The single sundowner on the veranda of the Company bungalow turns one evening into a double. A girl appears from among the flame trees, graceful, slant-eyed and compliant. He beckons, she mounts the veranda steps, slim, silent, with flowers in her hair.

Temple still felt the impact of shock when she had walked into Nick's bungalow and found a slim brown girl curled up on the cane divan, eating a mango, and gazing with imperturbable eyes at Temple as she asked in bewilderment if this was the house of Tuan Hallam.

'Nick out,' the girl had said in broken English. 'Trouble with boss man. Nick might get push from job—'

The girl had laughed, and then she had stopped laughing as Nick Hallam lurched into the untidy room. 'Out – go on, get out!' he had shouted at the girl. With a shrug, and a long look at Temple, the sarong-clad figure disappearing among the palms and the flame trees.

'W-why are you here?' Nick had asked.

'Because I thought you needed me.' Temple had looked him over and tried to see in his degenerate figure the gay young man who had promised her so much happiness. Temple Lane was sensitive, idealistic, all the things that an unloved orphan can't help becoming.

'Stay,' Nick had pleaded. 'I promise to change.'

She had taken a room at the hotel. She had tried to believe that Nick could straighten out. She had cleaned out his bungalow, met and talked to the manager of the big timber estate and won him a reprieve.

Things had begun to look brighter – until yesterday, when she had gone to the bungalow to prepare him a meal and found Lua there. The brown-gold girl in a scarlet wrap-around, locked in his arms.

Temple finished her pineapple juice and set the glass down with some deliberation. The hotel was quiet at this hour, with only the whirr of the fans and the low shrilling of the cicadas to disturb the heavy silence.

The steamer would be leaving in a couple of hours; starting out for Bangpalem as the day began to cool. Temple clenched her hands together on her lap, and the ring on her right hand held the only lustre in that drab

7

lounge. Her mother's engagement ring, set with a pearl ringed by garnets; Temple's only link with the parents she had lost when still a small child. Her Uncle Charles had been alive then, and life at Alford had not been too bad...

She sighed and knew she could not return to her aunt's house, to face the mockery of her cousins, and the monotony of the life there, which her job at the local library did not enlighten.

Bangpalem was the answer to her problem. Nick's manager had said there were big petroleum companies there, and that English secretaries were always welcome. There were a couple at the Sumica Oil Company right now, who had their own living quarters, and who earned very good money. Temple could type and take letters; she could do filing, and was strangely eager to stay out in the tropics. Its heavy scents, its lush foliage and sun-hot skies appealed to her. Alford in comparison seemed lifeless, promising nothing but a continuation of the life she had led there for most of her twenty-three years.

She wanted to get to Bangpalem as soon as possible... before Nick came to her and knocked down her defences again with his pleading and his promises.

She rose, slim-hipped as a boy in her cool blue dress. She picked up her suitcase and made her way to the powder room, as deserted as the hotel lounge, with a big mirror on the wall. Temple stared at herself in the mirror, and her pulse began to beat rather heavily.

Her smooth dark hair was cut short and it grew in a natural widow's peak at the centre of her forehead, above her wide hazel eyes. Her neck and her body had a vulnerable slenderness; her legs were long and slim with fleshless ankles. Her hands shook a little as she opened her raffia bag and took out the horn-rimmed spectacles which she wore for close work. She put them on and at

8

once they concealed the length of her lashes and the rather lost and girlish look which her eyes held.

She stared for long moments at herself and her heart thumped. In a jacket and a pair of slacks – with evening coming on – she could surely pass as a boy. She had no lush curves to betray her, only the pearl and garnet ring on her finger, which she now drew off and put carefully away in her purse.

Her decision was made as she drew off the ring. She would dress as a boy and try and get passage on the steamer. The clerk had said there was a spare berth . . . in a cabin that could only be shared by another male!

A demon of desperation seized hold of her. She unlocked her suitcase and took from it a pair of light slacks and her navy blazer with anchor buttons at either side. She still had the powder room to herself and it took her no more than ten minutes to slip out of her dress and into the boyish garb. She put on a thin white shirt with an open collar – passably masculine – and then the blazer, which she buttoned on the right side.

Again she studied her reflection and saw how pale and taut she looked – but undeniably boyish. She scrubbed off her pink lipstick and wiped a tissue over her face to remove any powder, then she replaced her horn-rimmed spectacles and assumed a frown that made her look suitably studious. Yes, Temple Lane – a youth – travelling to Bangpalem to take his first job at the Sumica Oil Company.

She stuffed her raffia bag into her suitcase, and then had a pang of alarm. Suppose they checked her luggage down at the quay! Oh lord, that would do it, if her suitcase was opened and they found frillies in it. She stood biting her lip. There was no airfield on Lumbaya, so flight by plane was not possible. She must either wait here another month for passage on the returned steamer, or she must take a chance on getting past the petty

9

officials at the quay without having her luggage checked.

Coming in on a steamer a month ago she had been checked on, but outgoing passengers, she had noticed, had received less attention. The officials had seemed more concerned with harassing the native population, who with bundles and baskets, and babies in slings, were leaving this small island for the rice fields of Bangpalem and other areas along the Sumatran coast.

She locked her suitcase, thrust the key in her pocket with purse, passport and visa, and made her way out of the powder room. She did not go to the clerk at the reception counter, but hurried towards the swing doors. There was a shipping agency along the street, the one the clerk had telephoned earlier in an effort to get her a passage on the steamer that was leaving today. It was the agency clerk who had said that the only berth available was that in the cabin – a large one – of Mijnheer van Helden.

There Temple's thoughts were shattered as she reached the street and saw Nick Hallam climbing out of a *trisha* in front of the hotel. She stood petrified as he paid off the boy and turned to come into the hotel. He had on a white tropical suit. He was shaved and his wavy hair was almost sleek. He came striding towards her, frowning, abstracted, and he almost bumped into her.

'Sorry, young feller.' He was gone without giving her a second glance, in through the swing doors, and the next moment Temple was racing along the street, thrusting her way past the people who were emerging from their houses after siesta. Spicy smells floated out from the open-fronted shops, there was a rising clang of traffic and the ping-ping of *trisha* bells.

Temple fled from Nick, from her moment of treacherous weakness. She had almost spoken his name, had nearly let herself in for more heartache, more disillusion, more scenes like the one she had witnessed yesterday at his bungalow.

He had come to the hotel to plead with her, and she had to get away before her old feeling for him weakened her resolve.

She entered the shipping office and stood a moment catching her breath. The clerk glanced up, a slim Javanese with the imperturbable eyes of the East. Those eyes flicked over her. 'Can I be of assistance to the *tuan*?' he asked. Temple, her heart beating very fast, approached the counter.

The quayside was crowded with the usual assortment of emigrating rice workers. The air was filled with noise from the tugs and barges, and the many mixed tongues. People jostled one another, and bundles swung at Temple as she fought her way to the gangplank that rose towards the deck of the steamer.

The customs man had given her passport a cursory glance. For a fearful moment his hand had hovered over her suitcase, then his attention had been caught by a Chinese whose bulging basket had burst open and was spilling rice seed all over the floor of the customs shed. Temple had been waved on her way while the official enjoyed himself bullying the rice farmer.

The water seethed beneath the gangplank as Temple made her way aboard the *Egret*. Some snow-white bird, with its smoky funnels and weathered frame, lurching to the swell as Temple stepped aboard.

This deck and the one below were crowded with passengers, hanging over the rail, waving to relatives on the dock. Babies cried and were hushed in the soft, sibilant tongue of the East. Men crouched over their bundles – all their worldly goods – and gazed at nothing with impenetrable eyes.

A strange scene, exciting, taking Temple's mind off her own worries for a while.

A rather coppery sun hung in the sky, dropping lower every few seconds until it painted the water and the sea-worn quay with a blush of rich colour. The gangplank was cleared and hoisted, and the shudder of the engines shook the steamer and there was a hiss, as of a cork pulling out of a bottle, as they began to churn through the copper-tinged water.

They were under way!

Temple leaned on the deck rail and felt the breeze blow through her hair. Ah, that felt good after a day of city heat and apprehension – not that everything was plain sailing now she had got aboard the steamer. There was still her fellow traveller to face!

She glanced along the deck, where groups of people were sitting down to eat a meal of rice and fish wrapped in a banana leaf. Many of them would sleep on deck tonight, spreading the mats in which their few posses-sions were bundled, gazed down upon by the stars that would soon appear now the sun had gone down. Wasn't it Eric Mackay who had said that the going down of the sun was like a wild confession of the moon?

Temple felt Asian eyes upon her as she lounged at the rail, and she had not been long enough in the tropics to have grown accustomed to the dark, mysterious stare of these people. Their reserve was deep within themselves, not the Façade behind which the English sheltered, and Temple picked up her suitcase and decided to go down and introduce herself – in the guise of a youth – to Mijnheer van Helden.

Would he be young or middle-aged? Would he be af-fable, or irritated at having to share his cabin with a stranger? She hoped that he would be disinterested. He was a Dutchman – a highly respected one, the shipping clerk had said – and he might not speak English.

She watched the passage of the wake, foam-ridged, tossing spray high over the stern, and was near the end of the deck when she almost lost her footing as the steamer rolled into a trough. She clutched at the deck rail and felt a sudden sensation of queasiness. The steamer seemed to be running into heavy seas, and Temple had never been a very good sailor as a child, when Uncle Charles used to take his family on boat outings at the seaside.

She breathed deeply, prayed that she was not going to be seasick, and descended the companionway to the cabin deck. The passage was dim and narrow, and Mijnheer's cabin was situated at the end of it. She tapped on the door. There was no answer and she entered, switching on the light by the door.

By steamer standards, she supposed, the cabin was fairly comfortable but not very large. A pigskin suitcase had been thrown on to the lower berth, but apart from that there were no other signs of Mijnheer's occupation – except perhaps a faint lingering tang of clove tobacco.

Temple climbed to the upper berth and put her suitcase at the foot of it. She lay back against the pillow, her arms behind her head, studying the ceiling and trying to fight that queasy little demon inside her. The cabin went up, then down, and she closed her eyes and suddenly hated Nick Hallam. If it had not been for him, she would not be masquerading as a youth on an old tub of a steamer somewhere on the Java seas.

She must have dozed off, and was awakened some time later by a flash that lit the cabin. Darkness fell again ... a sultry, blanketing darkness which told her that someone had been in and after leaving had switched off the light.

Again a lurid flash of lightning struck through the porthole, and Temple sat up in alarm.

They had run into a storm, one of those blue-white electric storms without rain. The seas were running high, and the heat had grown oppressive.

By the light of the flashes Temple felt her way down the wooden steps beside her berth to the dipping floor of the cabin. She felt in desperate need of some air, and she fought her way along the passage outside and mounted the iron stairs to the deck. People were huddled in groups along the deck, staring at the waves as they leapt the rails and sprayed the deck with moisture.

Temple clung to the rail and within seconds her hair was soaked and drops of water were running down her neck. She had removed her horn-rims in her berth, and she blinked her lashes at the rising onslaught and swayed to the rise and fall of the steamer. The deck planking seemed to groan and the thud of the engines was plain above the subdued Asian voices and the occasional sob of a frightened child.

The deck heaved and Temple did the same. Her face, her eyes, her lips were wet with spray. She wanted to curl up and die, and a few miserable tears mingled with the sea-water on her cheeks. Many times in her life had Temple felt alone, with no one to turn to, but never had that feeling been more potent than at the moment.

The creaking vessel was being mercilessly pounded by the waves, and Temple did not hear the approach of footsteps. She was aware dimly of a looming figure, and of a deep voice beside her. '*Niet lekker, mannetje?*'

It was a query, that was all she knew. She glanced up and in that moment the lightning played over the face of the man and she felt sure he must be one of the crew. He wore an eye-patch like a pirate – a silver-maned pirate of the Java seas!

'You are sick, eh?' Now he spoke in accented English. 'Not too good a storm, young man, therefore it would be better if you went below.'

'I – I prefer to stay here,' she gasped, for her legs could not be trusted to carry her down the companion-way to the cabin. 'I – I shall be all right—'

'I think not.' She was taken hold of and urged along the deck, now slippery with water, and when she stumbled a strong pair of arms lifted her and she was carried down the iron stairway, the whip of the wind lashing her to this big sailor who carried her like an infant to the Mijnheer's cabin. He pushed open the door and a thrust of his elbow flicked on the light. She felt the flick of a light grey eye, and then she was carried across the cabin and laid in the lower berth.

'No,' she said weakly, 'this is not my berth—'

'Be quiet, *mannetje*.'

She now felt too woeful and weary to argue with him, and she watched with stunned eyes as he opened the Mijnheer's pigskin suitcase and took from it a silver flask. He unscrewed it and forced a little of the brandy between her lips, and then took a swig himself.

'Sh-should you do that?' she whispered.

'Should I do what?' That grey eye was singularly disturbing set beside that triangular dark patch. A sea-coloured eye, vivid in the sun and wind-browned face.

'Make free of Mijnheer van Helden's brandy,' she said, a little revived by it, but heavy-eyed and ready to fall off to sleep any minute.

He studied her, narrowing that sea-grey eye as he took in her seal-wet hair and her pale face against the pillow. He was very tall, hard-featured, and it was the lightning that had made his hair seem silvery. Here beneath the cabin light it was a tawny mane, sea-wet and clinging to his broad forehead. His jutting nose was that of a man of strong will-power, and decision.

Something – perhaps a smile – gleamed in his grey eye, and then he bowed in a totally foreign way and said arrogantly: 'Ryk van Helden at your service. The cognac is mine, also the berth in which you lay. You are the young *Inglese* who shares this cabin with me – *ach*, your eyes droop, you are almost asleep, so stay where you are.'

'Mijnheer—' She struggled to say more, to rise, but he put a large hand against her shoulder and pushed her back against the pillow. She felt his fingers press the bones of her shoulder.

'You are not a very robust young man.' His smile was mocking.

She saw his face through a haze of tiredness – a strong, formidable face, made a little sinister by the eye-patch. Ryk van Helden, with whom she would share this cabin through the stormy night.

'I am sure, *meneer*,' she said with her last ounce of spirit, 'that muscles are not all that makes the man.'

He quirked a tufted eyebrow and stood braced against the rock and roll of the cabin floor. The last thing Temple remembered was his looming figure as he drew off her blazer and put up a hand to adjust the netting about the berth in which she lay. Then everything faded and she slept. . . .

CHAPTER TWO

THE storm had died away and the light of morning lay serene over the Java Sea.

Temple opened her eyes as a streak of sun thrust its way through the porthole of the cabin. She stretched drowsily and blinked her lashes ... and then she sat up and thrusting aside the netting gazed wonderingly around the small cabin and felt the steady throbbing of a boat's engines.

Of course, she was on board the *Egret,* a steamer outward bound from Lumbaya and heading for islands scattered like jewels in the Java Sea.

The sheet slipped from her shoulders as she remembered this, and sudden consternation swept over her as she realized that she was clad in the large jade-silk jacket of a pair of male pyjamas!

She fingered the wide sleeves and remembered the man who had carried her to this cabin last night ... it was he who had whipped off her damp clothes, thinking he undressed a youth. She bit her lip and felt a warmth in her cheeks. It must have come as quite a shock to him to find he had undressed a girl ... were not Dutchmen said to be rather puritanical?

At that moment someone tapped on the door of the cabin, then it opened decisively and Ryk van Helden came striding in. Temple didn't know where to put her face. Her fingers clenched the sheet, and she shrank instinctively against the wall of the berth as the sun struck his mane of hair, and the whiteness of the shirt beneath which his shoulders stretched, powerful, flagrantly male.

'*Goede morgen,*' he said in Dutch. 'You slept well?'

She nodded and tried to read his face, but who could read the expression of a man who had one light grey eye and a dark patch over the other one?

He placed across her lap the tray he carried. There was a pot of coffee on it, also rolls, butter and fruit. 'I thought you would prefer a light breakfast, *meisje*.'

'Thank you.' She pondered the word he had used as she poured her coffee into a cup like a small bowl. 'You have breakfasted, *meneer*?'

'An hour ago.' He stretched his large frame in a wicker chair and watched her as she sipped her coffee. She was acutely aware that he was taking in the delicate definition of her temple and the line of her cheek.

'Do eat a *broodje*,' he said in his deep, accented voice. 'You look quite pale, *meisje*.'

'I – I suppose you are waiting for an explanation—' She looked at him and felt her heart beat nervously.

'Yes, it would interest me to know why you dress as a boy – you realize that I removed your clothes because I found them to be damp. The eastern climate can be cruel to the *sinkeh* who does not take care.'

'There was room for one more passenger on the steamer—' Her hazel eyes met his disconcerting light and dark gaze. 'The shipping clerk said you would share your cabin, but there would have been no chance of that if I – I had not dressed as a boy—'

'You think not?' he drawled. He looked her over, young and pale-skinned in his silk pyjama jacket. 'What an innocent you are! Only an innocent would resort to the folly of such a masquerade – were you running away from a man?'

'Yes,' she admitted. 'I had to get away from Lumbaya I couldn't stay there another month—'

'I quite understand. Now you will eat some food.' It was an order and she obeyed him, her eyes downcast as she buttered a *broodje* and nibbled it. She heard a match strike, and then the tang of a clove cigarette floated across to her. He towered to his feet and went to look out of the porthole.

'The day will be a fine one after the storm,' he said. 'You are travelling to Bangpalem, I understand?'

'Yes.' She sliced a papaya and as always the pale green inner fruit surprised her with its sweetness. 'A timber boss at Lumbaya told me that I would get secretarial work at the Sumica Oil Company.'

'Ah, you are a secretary?' Ryk van Helden swung round to look at her. 'That is interesting.'

'Really?' Her smile was sceptical. 'I am sure you know all about this part of the Indies, *meneer*. Do you think I will get work at Bangpalem?'

'So long as you do not intend to carry on with your masquerade,' he said drily. 'It has its dangers – as you have already learned.'

She felt the silk of his pyjama jacket against her skin, and colour rose in her cheeks. Never in her life had she felt more aware of being a woman, for never in her life before had she met a man like Ryk van Helden. A tawny tiger of a man with a faintly mocking mouth.

'What are you looking at – my disfigurement?' He lifted his cigarette and drew on it. 'Does it make me appear sinister, a bold *vrijbuiter* of the high seas?'

'I don't understand the word,' she said.

'It means freebooter.' He tapped ash off his clove cigarette with a long finger, and his smile deepened the lines that the tropical sun had etched into his face. 'I manage the plantations of a Javanese prince. Tea, tobacco, and teak. I am on my way home to Bayanura after a business trip which was rather unsatisfactory from my point of view.'

He strolled to the door and there he spoke over his shoulder. 'We will meet on deck in an hour. Please to dress as a boy for the remainder of the voyage, unless

you wish to arrive at Bangpalem with a rather tar-
nished reputation.'

The door closed behind him, but the tang of his tobacco
remained, along with his parting remark. Temple mulled
it over in her mind and came to the conclusion that no
one in Bangpalem would be likely to believe that Ryk
van Helden would innocently share a steamer cabin
with a girl. With that air of arrogance, those wide
shoulders, and that eye-patch, he was obviously looked
upon as every bit as dangerous as he appeared.

Temple slipped hurriedly out of her berth, her legs
long and slim beneath the jade-silk pyjama jacket. Mijnheer van Helden had a taste for the exotic, she thought,
as she took down her suitcase from the upper berth and
breathed the lingering scent of clove tobacco.

The steamer thrust its way through the glittering blue-
green water. Tiny waves melted together and the sea
was like crêpe; overhead the sun burned behind a haze of
gold.

'We are but fish in the Indies' spangled net,' said a
deep voice above her head.

She turned to look at the Dutchman, and she felt less
at a disadvantage now she was clad in her slacks and
blazer. She wore her horn-rims and her hair sprang
youthfully from her widow's peak. A smile quivered on
her mouth. 'I think you are a rather big fish in the Indies,
meneer. I have never met before a man who worked for
a prince – it sounds exotic.'

He lounged against the rail with his wide shoulders to
the sea. His hair reflected the sun like raw gold . . . though
his hair was so fair, his skin was bronze as autumn-
burned leaves. So deep was the cleft in his chin that it
might have been chiselled there. There was an air of
dominancy about him; a sheer and utter maleness.

'I am the *tuan besar* of the island; answerable to the

prince only,' he said. 'I even live in the *kraton*.'

'What is a *kraton*?' she asked curiously.

'A palace.' His grey eye held a wicked gleam. 'A peacock palace, where those jewel-tailed birds strut in the courtyard with their harems of peahens.'

'And you, *meneer*?' she said daringly. 'As lord of an island, have you a harem?'

She thought he would smile, for she only jested, but instead a sudden harshness etched his mouth. 'That is none of your business,' he said curtly.

'Then tell me some more about the island.' His voice had flicked like a whip, and Temple knew that she had opened a wound in this man who was outwardly so cool and hard.

'Once upon a time the island was a possession of the Dutch; a part of the Netherlands Indies. An ancestress of mine used to call it the isle of a thousand fragrances – but that was in the days when the Dutch were masters of much of the Indies; when the tide ran golden for them.' He turned upon Temple a brooding look. 'Then the Japanese invaded and a darkness fell over the islands. After the war there was a rebellion and the Dutch were no longer the kings of these seas.'

'But you are here, *meneer*.'

'I was here as a very small child. When my parents were taken prisoner, an old Javanese servant of theirs took me to live among her people. They dyed my hair and fed and cared for me. I grew up in a palm-thatched house and I learned – in short I learned to love the islanders.'

A moment of silence brooded, and then Temple said gently: 'What became of your parents?'

'They were separated, sent to different camps. My father, along with hundreds of other Dutch colonials, was marched all the way to Manchuria, where he died after a crude operation on feet and legs covered with infected blisters. The war ended and I was reunited with my mother, but not for long. The life in an internment camp had taken too much toll of her and she died during the revolt that swept the Indies. The winds of change, *meisje*. They carried me home to Leyden to my mother's people, but I could never forget the Indies and the golden islands.'

His heavy seal ring caught the sun as he closed a hand over the rail where they stood side by side. 'I met Prince Chai at university in Holland. When he learned of my interest in the islands, and of my years as a boy among his people, he suggested that I take on the management of his plantations at Bayanura. That was ten years ago. Neither of us has had cause for regret.'

Temple felt stirred, by his story, and by his love for the Indies. Its beauty was seducing her, and she was but a newcomer. A world of blue skys and peacock waters, behind which a typhoon might lurk. Of exotic temples and kampongs. The spell of the tiger, and the menace of the volcano.

'And you are a secretary,' he said suddenly.

'A librarian really, but I'm accustomed to typing and filing.' She glanced up at him and was struck by the intent way he was looking down at her. He stirred and took a sudden deep breath.

'You wish very much to work at the Sumica Oil Company?'

'I need a job, *meneer*. The money I saved to come out here has almost run out—' She broke off and bit her lip. 'I have been told that Sumica employ European secretaries, and I think I should like to work in the tropics for a while.'

'For two months, say?'

She looked at him and began to feel strangely excited. 'Yes, *meneer*. In that time I should have saved enough to return to England – should I want to return.

The spangled net has meshes that cling.'

'Do you think,' he paused and turned to watch a hawk in motion above the glittering sea, a dark-winged etching, 'you would like working for me for about two months?'

She could only look at him and could not imagine what sort of work he had in mind – if it was work he had in mind!

'I read your thoughts.' There was a rather sardonic quirk to his lips as he looked at her. 'I know what you are thinking, and wondering, but let me assure you that all I need is a proficient typist – I have no designs on your virtue.'

She flushed and thought how cruel he could sound, and look. 'I am sorry, *meneer*—'

'There is a saying, that to judge from appearances is to raise tigers. Or then again you could be confusing me with the man you are running away from. Were you working for him?'

She tautened, there beside the deck rail, and felt hotly inclined to tell Mijnheer van Helden to mind his own business. The impulse flared and died. 'I hoped to marry him,' she said frigidly. 'Instead I learned that I had fallen in love with an idea rather than a reality. That my shining knight in a white suit was an illusion. It has shaken my belief in people.'

'You are young. You have plenty of time in which to recover from a broken *dream*.' He spoke the word contemptuously, and her eyes widened, her lips shook sensitively.

'There is one thing for certain,' she said. 'You've never been in love enough to be hurt.'

He forbore to answer her, instead he looked at her frosty-eyed. 'You are impulsive, and in danger of falling headlong in love again, if you are not careful. Now about this work I wish to have done. Do you think you could type into manuscript form a number of diaries written many years ago by an ancestress of mine?'

'But I have no knowledge of the Dutch language, *meneer.*'

'The diaries are in English,' he explained. 'Polyana van Helden was an English girl who entered into a glove marriage with Laurens van Helden.'

'A glove marriage?' Temple looked fascinated.

'A marriage by proxy.' A smile twitched on his lips as he opened his cigarette case and held it out to her. 'Do you smoke, *meisje*?'

She shook her head. 'Do tell me more about this marriage, *meneer*. Was it a happy one?'

He puffed a cloud of fragrant smoke and quizzed her upraised face. 'The story of the marriage is in the diaries, for Polyana had a gift for words and she filled many of them in her forty years with Laurens van Helden. Many glove marriages were made in those days, when adventurous young men left the Netherlands to live and work in the Indies. A young and lonely Dutchman would apply to the Indies Company for a bride, and he would send to her a jewelled glove scented with cinnamon and cloves. She would sail out to him, bringing with her the glove she had worn during the ceremony by proxy.'

'But a man she had never met!' Temple removed her horn-rims absently, and her eyes looked very large and wondering.

'Polyana was a vital young creature, the stepdaughter of a Hague merchant who feared that she was outshining his own daughters. The girl was unhappy at home, and she had also an adventurous spirit, so she agreed to this marriage with a man she had never met.'

'A marriage that lasted forty years,' Temple murmured. 'Then it could not have been an unhappy one, not if Polyana wished to write about her husband and his family history.'

'The diaries are most interesting to read, and though I could send them away to be typed, they are valuable to me and I wish the work to be done at Bayanura, in the surroundings known and loved by Polyana.'

'They are to be published, *meneer*?'

He nodded. 'That is one of the reasons why I wish to check on the manuscript as it grows. I interviewed a secretary at Lumbaya, who had worked for a timber company there, but it turned out that her knowledge of English was not sufficient for the task. She was Asian, you understand.'

'You feel, Mijnheer van Helden, that I would be proficient at the task?' The idea alarmed Temple, and yet she felt excited by the prospect of living and working for two months on a tropical isle.

He quizzed her through his cigarette smoke, a man who looked every inch the descendant of bold navigators who sailed the seas in great ships and founded island empires – a cruel and golden age. 'I feel that you as an English girl alone in the tropics will understand Polyana and the early dilemmas that must have faced her as the bride of a stranger. Work is all the better done if an enthusiasm for it is there.'

'I – I do rather like the idea,' she admitted.

'Then why do you hesitate?' He flicked ash over the rail and the seal of his heavy ring caught the sun. 'You dared to dress as a youth in order to get passage on this steamer – does it take more courage to come to Bayanura as my secretary?'

'It's something I must carefully consider,' she said.

'You have only a matter of hours in which to do that,' he spoke drily, with an underlying note of impatience. 'Later this afternoon a boat from the island will take me off the steamer – Bayanura lies off the direct route to Bangpalem.'

'Then if I agreed to work there, it would not be easy

25

for me to get away?' She replaced her horn-rims, for they made her feel more businesslike, less of a girl alone in the Indies, one who felt herself poised on the rim of a strange – and inviting – danger.

There was a rather cruel little quirk to his lips as he sized her up. 'If you are hesitating because you fear I shall lose my head over being alone with you, then let me put your fears at rest. In the first place you are not my type; in the second you will be given your own house in which to live. Furthermore an American doctor flies to the island once a week in order to hold a surgery at our small bamboo clinic. Any time you felt like running away again, I am sure Kinraid would be only too happy to take you as a passenger.'

Her cheeks stung, and so did her eyes for a moment. She wanted to retort that she had been only too ready to love Nick with warmth and gratitude – there had been too little love in her life for her to be proud. But Nick had not wanted her because he loved her; he had needed someone to fight his battles for him.

'Well,' he tossed overboard the end of his cigarette, 'does my proposition now take on a different aspect?'

'Yes, a much more attractive one,' she said tartly. 'What would you pay me?'

He told her, and though she was far from mercenary it was a wage she would be a fool to turn down. 'Why,' she asked, 'could not Dr. Kinraid have brought you a secretary from Bangpalem? I have been told that European girls are employed there.'

'Yes, Europeans work there and it is a hive of gossip, and petty affairs and scandals. I prefer to employ someone who has not a taste for such things – someone who will approach the typing of the diaries with interest and respect.'

'I could be running away from an affair, *meneer*.'

He laughed and thrust a hand through his mane of

hair, so alive in the sun. In his white ducks and open-necked shirt he looked a picture of vigour – a man with a tiger lurking beneath that sun-toughened skin. 'You are not the type for affairs, *meisje*. You want marriage, security, and even love as well.'

'You speak very cynically, *meneer*.' She looked directly at him. 'Like a man who doesn't believe in love.'

'On the contrary,' he drew himself up to his full and formidable height. 'I know that love exists, but I know also that once lost it is rarely found again. Now permit me to tell you a little more about our way of life on Bayanura.'

She listened to him, and yet had half her mind on the mystery of the man. A strong, self-reliant type, yet he had been hurt – to her surprise – by the promise or the loss of love.

She listened to the deep, accented voice of Ryk van Helden, and felt the motion of the steamer through the peacock water, and she knew with a kind of inevitability that there was no turning back to Nick, no going on to Bangpalem. She wanted to go to Bayanura and work on the diaries of Polyana van Helden – glove bride of a man who must have looked very much as Ryk looked.

Gods of the colonies they had been called in the old days. Men who tamed the seas and the tropics. Men who were loved . . . or hated.

'There is a tennis-court in the palace gardens,' Ryk was saying, and there he broke off as a scuffle suddenly ensued among some Asians playing a game of cards further along the deck. There was a scream from a woman as a knife flashed, and then in three strides Ryk was across the deck and Temple watched in a kind of fascination as he took hold of the man's wrist and deliberately bent it backwards until the *kris* fell point down into the hot planking of the deck. The Asian nursed his wrist and groaned, and Ryk said something in the Asian dialect that subdued the group before the mate of the steamer appeared.

'*Dag*!' Ryk van Helden strolled back to Temple as if nothing had happened. A grubby hand had marked his white ducks, that was all, and he was thrusting a strand of hair back from his eye-patch.

'You look pale, *meisje*.' He towered over her. 'Emotions are easily aroused in the tropics, and they have to be dealt with swiftly.'

'And ruthlessly, I notice.' She drew back against the deck rail, aware through all her being of the tiger in this man. 'You near enough broke the fellow's wrist.'

'Better his wrist askew than his neck.' The broad shoulders lifted on a shrug. 'You are a newcomer to the Indies. You cannot be expected to understand that always there is a mute menace in the air of the tropics – look at the sea! Today like silk, yet beneath surges the forces of storm and danger. If these things frighten you, *meisje*, then you would do better to return to England. If you have run out of money, I will pay your fare—'

'No!' It wasn't exactly a cry of pride, of not wanting to take money from this man, it was that he had challenged her spirit of adventure. 'No, *meneer*, I should like to accept your offer of work. I'm used to handling books, and Polyana intrigues me—'

'Why?' He quirked one of those bold eyebrows. 'Because she married a man she had never met?'

'I suppose so.' Temple watched the creaming wake of the steamer, and her heartbeats quickened. She had made her choice, and that afternoon would leave the steamer in the company of a man she had known less than a day.

'Don't worry.' That sardonic note was back in Ryk van Helden's voice. 'Unlike Laurens I need a secretary but have no desire for a wife.'

28

Temple glanced up into the sun-toughened face with its decisive features and clefted chin, and its shadow of a painful memory. If it had not been for that, she would have retorted that after Nick Hallam she had no intention of falling in love again ... least of all with a man who had known someone he could not forget. One dose of disillusion out here in the tropics was too bitter to repeat.

'Come.' Hard brown fingers took her by the elbow. 'Let us go down to the saloon and have some lunch. The Captain's rice-table is not as good as that you will taste on Bayanura, but it will suffice, and you must be feeling hungry.'

She was, surprisingly enough.

CHAPTER THREE

THE sea was liquid gold and the high-peaked prow of the boat was painted with a single eye. The broad swing of the paddles made a molten spray as they were rowed to the island, a green and feathery mass with the blue-veiled cone of a volcano rising in a spectacular way towards the sky.

Bayanura, a pagan island of timeless beauty, with outlying coral beds and ridges of reef, where clouds of rainbow fish darted. The sea had gnawed gaps in the cliffs, and as they drew nearer at every stroke of the paddles, Temple saw the white beach and the great banyan trees, their branches sweeping down to the ground in a kind of prolific obeisance.

She felt Ryk van Helden's glance, but could not speak for the ache in her throat. It was all so strangely beautiful beneath the waning sun, with small waves fire-tipped as they beat against the cliffs. She felt herself bewitched . . . and knew that in this way Polyana had been rowed to the island, apprehensive of the man at her side, and the life ahead of her.

A small stone jetty loomed ahead of them, and a cluster of islanders stood beneath the banyans and the towering palms. The people of the *tuan besar*, come to greet him after his absence from home. Temple felt their quick dark eyes summing her up as Ryk helped her to alight. His hand, lean-fingered, work-hardened, squeezed her fingers as if to reassure her, then he gave his attention to the leaders of the village, and to the women who greeted him with a graceful bow over slender fingertips placed together.

He introduced Temple to them. The *nonya* who had

come to assist with the work on the history of the island, of his people and theirs, recorded in the diaries of Mevrouw Polyana.

'*Ah*—!' a sibilant indrawing of breath, and dawning glances of respect were cast at Temple. A lady of learning . . . for all that she looked like a boy!

She smiled shyly in return and walked among them with Ryk, a slow, ceremonial procession that wended its way up the beach and in among the tall trees festooned with scarlet creepers. The women wore long wraparound skirts in gay colours, with tunics of silk. Ear pendants hung from their earlobes, and bracelets and chains tinkled on their slender arms. They had dressed in their finery to greet Ryk, who towered above them and the men in his tropical whites, very much the lord of the island in the absence of Prince Chai.

Twilight breathed and died – night fell as they came to the pillared entrance of the peacock palace. They were escorted as far as the lantern-lit courtyard, and then their escort melted away and Temple found herself alone with the man who lived among these sweeping arcades, these cool high rooms, and gushes of scented flowers.

All around them breathed 'the thousand-eyed night of the East'. Lotus-blossoms closed their petals in the ponds, and the lanterns hung like heavy blossoms among the trees.

Suddenly in the stillness there was a screech, and Temple caught at Ryk's arm. 'What was that?'

'One of the peacocks.' The lantern light was strange on his face; that triangular patch of darkness made him sinister. 'Beautiful birds, but they should have been made just to be looked at – unlike the nightingale.'

They were bowed into the tiled hall of the palace by a pair of white-coated servants, and Temple entered as in a dream. The air seemed faintly redolent of spices and musky blossoms. She saw the *melati* blossoms massed in bowls, and then the stone figure of a goddess with jade eyes and a contemplative expression. 'Kwan Yin, goddess of mercy.' Ryk touched the idol with his hand, the sinews stretched taut beneath the brown skin. He was a little tense, Temple realized, as if not for a long while had a European girl set foot in this exotic home of his.

'She looks so peaceful.' Even Temple's low and naturally husky voice picked up echoes from the marble arcades. *Melati* petals had fallen to the coloured tiles, and pagoda cabinets gleamed in the shadows with mother-of-pearl inlay. Soft Indian rugs lay here and there on the floor, and set among the Colonial Dutch furniture were screens painted with peacocks and strange flowers. Carved teakwood doors led into various rooms, and a fountain tinkled softly in the centre of the hall.

'It's all very grand,' said Temple, looking about with shy and fascinated eyes as the servants carried trays of food to a low circular table set in an alcove. Silver bowls were placed so that Temple and her host could wash their hands, which were then dried by the servants on embroidered towels. Temple caught Ryk's eye and saw a gleam of amusement in it.

'Please be seated at my table, Juffrouw Temple,' he said formally. 'I have an excellent cook and you will find the food very tasty.'

They sat in low chairs with high backs, and the main dish was a chicken steamed in lotus leaves, aromatic with a herb and chestnut filling, placed on a tray carved like a lotus-leaf, and set round with small bowls of rice, plain or spiced, diced vegetables and sauces.

Mijnheer carved the tender chicken, and Temple helped herself to rice and vegetables. 'Do you always dine in such splendour?' she asked, fingering the long stem of the glass into which his servant had poured a cool, gold wine.

'A hard-working planter is permitted an indulgence or two. Mmm, this chicken is delicious!'

He ate with appetite and encouraged Temple to do the same, and at the end of the meal he took her into a small *sala* to show her the diaries of Polyana van Helden. 'She started the first one during the long sea voyage from Holland,' he said as he unlocked a lovely old lacquer box and revealed the diaries, each one bound in leather and stamped with the van Helden seal.

A musty scent of cloves mingled with Ryk's cigar smoke as he unclasped the very first diary in which Polyana had recorded her feelings of apprehension and hope during the long days of a sailing ship which had dared the dangerous waters in which Spanish and Portuguese pirate ships had lurked.

'Will he love me?' Ryk read out in his deep, accented voice. 'Like everyone I carry in my heart an image of the person I could love. I have been sent a miniature of Laurens – even to write his name causes my pulse to quicken with apprehension – but I cannot tell from looking at his brown face, his fair hair and grey eyes whether he is a man I could care for. His eyes are like the sea, and not all seas are warm in the tropics, some are cold and filled with storm. Each time I take out the miniature to study the face of my husband – how intimate a word to use about a man I have never met! – I am a little chilled by his look of reserve and arrogance. He has bought a bride in the marriage market, and I pray that he will not regret his choice when at last we meet. I carry to him his jewelled glove, which I wore at the ceremony. It is adorned with real garnets and pearls, and silver-thread initials – his and mine.'

Ryk closed the diary and glanced deep into Temple's eyes, lucent as honey in that moment. 'You like the sound of Polyana, eh?' He went to a lacquered cabinet in a corner of the lamplit room and opened one of the

drawers painted with butterflies and birds and twisted trees of Asian antiquity. He took from it a little box,
and something wrapped in silk.

He brought them to Temple, his cigar clamped
between his teeth and wreathing smoke. He opened the
box and took from it a pair of miniatures, one set in plain
silver, the other in gold and seed pearls, and handed them
to Temple. 'The miniature of Laurens which Polyana
carried on the voyage, and one of Polyana herself,
painted when she had been married two years.'

Temple held the miniatures and studied them by one
of the lamps. Yes, her instinct had been right. Laurens
had looked much as Ryk would look if he were not dis-
figured by a blind eye. Polyana had been a vital-looking
girl, with Vermeer-blue eyes and chestnut hair – and the
smile of someone very much loved.

'I can't wait to begin work on the diaries.' Temple
glanced at Ryk and saw that he was unfolding the square
of silk. She held her breath as he disclosed the jewelled
and velvet glove which Laurens had sent to Polyana,
and which she had worn to marry him by proxy. The
cuff was encrusted with garnets and pearls, real ones
which had not lost too much of their lustre down the
years. The L and the P were closely woven together in
silverwork.

'May I – may I try on the glove?' Temple asked breathlessly.

That light and dark glance flashed over her face.
'There is a superstition that if a single girl tries on such a
glove she will remain a spinster,' Ryk warned her.

'I'm fully prepared for that,' Temple said, with more
lightness than she felt. 'Love can be too disillusioning.'

'All the same,' a smile flickered on his lips, 'just place
your hand against the glove – ah, you have a small hand,
meisje. No doubt Polyana's hand was lost in the glove.'

'It's very beautiful.' Temple traced the silver initials

with a fingertip. 'I suppose in those days the fate of spinsterhood was considered a dire one.'

'But it does not strike you as a dire one, eh?'

She glanced up at Ryk and with the jewelled glove between them she felt less tense, less overwhelmed by the strong personality of the man. The lamplight was kind to his tough brown face, with the edge of a scar showing beneath that triangular dark patch. How had he lost the eye, and when?

'This man at Lumbaya hurt you badly, *meisje*?'

She nodded. 'Perhaps I expected too much of him, but if he didn't really love me, then he should not have kept on writing to me. I – I built a seven-storey pagoda for myself, and found I built it of paper.'

'What of your people in England?' Ryk lounged against the carved table on which stood a portable type-writer. 'Will they worry now you have left this man and yet remain here?'

She couldn't help but give a broken little laugh. 'I am another Polyana, *meneer*. I lived with an aunt and some cousins who thought I was there to be useful rather than liked – liked at least, for they were never a very loving family.

'I see.' Cigar smoke came strong from his arched nostrils. 'It was that, or chance marriage with this man at Lumbaya, but unlike Polyana you were not so fortun-ate in your choice of a bridegroom. Was it drink, or another woman?'

'Both,' she said, and went round the table to take a look at the typewriter. It was a new one, and beside it was stacked manuscript paper, carbon in a box, a pad for taking notes and several ball-point pens. 'Shall I be working here at the palace in this room, *meneer*?'

'Yes. In the mornings this room catches a lot of sun-shine and light and overlooks a small flower garden where you can take your *breken*. There are books here,' he indicated them with a sweep of his cigar, 'which you may need to refer to. Our Dutch past has been a splendid one, perhaps a cruel one, but always interesting.'

'I believe the Dutch and the English were fierce enemies at one time.' Temple looked at him with a faint air of challenge, as if to let him know that she was not like the graceful, submissive island women, bowing like temple dancers over their fingertips down on the beach. To them he was entirely the *tuan besar*. To her he was a boss during working hours only.

He bowed sardonically, the point taken. 'You will not find me officious,' he drawled. 'I am away from the *kraton* much of the day, for there is always much to supervise. The tea, the tobacco, and the timber, not to mention the rice terraces and the tropical fruits. I keep busy *meisje*.'

'Prince Chai must be a wealthy man,' she said. 'Does he ever come to Bayanura to look at his plantations?'

'Now and again he pilots his own small plane and surprises us with a visit. You are curious about him?'

'Naturally. He's a Javanese prince, and I worked in a library and handled many romantic novels.' She smiled and recalled moments of longing at Alford for the sunshine and tousled palm trees by a tropical shore. 'I am not exactly the ideal heroine to look at, but my surroundings are certainly romantic.'

'You are among the people of the long day-dream.' He quizzed her pointed, wide-eyed face as he bent to a brass bell on the writing-table and gave it a shake. 'I think we must drink to your working visit to Bayanura, and then I will take you to your *huisje*.'

One of his silent-footed servants entered and Ryk spoke to him in the soft, sibilant dialect of the island. Ranji withdrew, and Temple gave Ryk an inquiring look. 'What is a – a *huisje*?'

'A little house.' He strolled to the lacquer cabinet and put away the miniatures and the jewelled glove. 'A

Javanese teahouse which has been converted into a guest bungalow, and which stands in the gardens of the palace. I am sure you will find it pleasant, and also you will have a house girl of your own.'

'A Javanese teahouse!' Temple's imagination quickened to the idea of living in so quaint a house, set in the palace gardens, lush with tropical trees and plants.

Ranji carried in a tray on which stood a squat bottle and a pair of lovely old goblets. He set down the tray, bowed and withdrew, and Temple watched the lamplight on Ryk's face as he poured a measure of liqueur into each goblet.

'Here you are.' Ryk handed her one of the goblets and raised his own. 'May the palace of peacocks restore to you some of your lost illusions, *meisje*.'

'Thank you, *meneer*.' The liqueur was exotic and strong, a blend of island fruits and raw gold sunshine, leaving Temple a little heady.

'Come.' They made their way from the *sala* into the garden itself, and he took a lantern from the wall and led her into the heart of the gardens to the teahouse set among a grove of musky tamarinds and clove-trees.

Temple walked at Ryk's side as though in a strange dream, and her breath caught in her throat when suddenly she was caught within the embrace of a trailing liana. Warm, hard fingertips touched her as she was set free, and the musky scents, the liqueur, rushed to her head and she felt weak with a frightening urge to touch Ryk van Helden. To touch the strong face, the ravaged eye, the broad shoulders – she drew sharply away from him as he released her from the liana, and heard him draw in his breath through his proud, arching nostrils.

'It is like a small jungle, eh? A living thing that knows you a stranger.' He thrust aside the flowering creepers and there stood the teahouse, lit by lanterns along its deep veranda.

37

Temple squared her slim shoulders and took in the house in which she would live while she worked for Ryk van Helden. She heard a soft tinkling as they approached the steps of the veranda and saw wind-bells shine in the lantern light, suspended on chains from the carved eaves of the pagoda roof.

A slight figure came out softly from the house. A girl clad in Chinese trousers and a tunic, who placed her hands together and bowed first to the *tuan* and then to Temple.

'This is Mei.' Ryk gave the girl a smile not seen before by Temple; it was gentle, almost, holding the indulgence of the strong towards the fragile – a girl fragile as a bamboo stem as she stood, hands still clasped in front of her, and gazed with tilting dark eyes at Temple.

Ryk spoke to the girl in Dutch and she smiled and bobbed her head and backed into the house. 'Mei is from Singapore,' he explained 'She speaks a little Dutch and even a smattering of English, but is very shy. She was working as a little coolie girl and had no real home when I found her. She can cook and sew, and will serve you quietly and pleasantly. Mei Flower, she is rather like one, eh?'

'Asian girls do have a gift for grace,' Temple agreed, and she gave a slight shiver as the wind-bells tinkled and a night breeze rustled the fronds of the palms and the casuarina trees. The breeze touched the nape of Temple's neck like the brush of cold fingers.

'Nervous?' Ryk must have felt the shiver that had run through her. 'There is no need to be. That husky croaking comes from the tree *kikkers*, and that whispering from the long leaves of the casuarinas brushing against each other. Soon you will grow used to the island at night and will come to recognize its many voices and its thousand scents.'

Temple took a deep breath of those mingling scents.

'There is one scent that seems extra potent,' she said. 'It comes from that corner of the compound.'

'The datura,' he said. 'The islanders believe that it has magical powers. They have been known to make love potions from the pollen.'

She smiled cynically, and thought of the island girl who had put blossoms in her long dark hair to enchant Nick Hallam. 'I am not nervous of the whispering trees, *meneer*. It's people I have grown wary of.'

'People are not always easy to know.' He leaned back against the teakwood support of the veranda, a tall figure in the shadowy lantern light. 'But understanding was never won without a battle or two.'

'You are expecting one or two battles with me, *meneer*?' She plucked a leaf from an overhanging camphor tree and crushed it between her fingers. The scent that arose was spiced ... like this conversation in the night with a man who was so individual, a little mysterious.

'A clash of ideas and opinions is inevitable,' he said dryly. 'You are a woman. I am a man.'

'I had you fooled for a while, *meneer*.' She laughed, and then broke off as he leaned forward suddenly and she caught his wicked glimmer of a smile.

'What would you say, *meisje*, if I admitted now that I was not fooled by your disguise for longer than a moment?'

She caught her breath. 'You – you put me into your pyjama jacket, thinking I was a boy!'

'I knew you were not a boy when I carried you down to the cabin. Appearances can be deceptive, *meisje*, but not touch.'

Her cheeks flamed in the half-dark. 'You had no right to!'

'I could certainly have left you to sleep damp and invite a fever.' He drew himself up to his full height. 'What does it matter? A man of thirty-three knows what a woman looks like!'

'That's all very well—'

'*Het spijt me*,' he said mockingly. 'Next time I will let you keep your modesty – in any case, to me you are just a *kindje*.'

'A – and what it that?' she asked stiffly.

'A child. One who needs her bed if she is to be a capable *secretaresse* in the morning.'

'You are infuriating—' Then she gave a reluctant laugh. 'You said we would fight.'

'Of course.'

'The *tuan besar* is always right, is that it?'

'He tries to be.' A sardonic bow. 'Follow the *laan* through the trees in the morning and it will bring you to the palace.'

'How do I thank you in Dutch for my job, *meneer*?'

'*Dankbaar* is what you say.'

'Then *dankbaar, meneer*. I am most grateful for work I know I shall enjoy.'

'*Goede nacht, meisje.*'

She watched his tall figure disappear among the trees, and stood a moment on the veranda savouring the strangeness of this place ... a teahouse in a tropical garden. Place of mysterious beauty and low teeming sounds, and a feeling of brooding passion.

CHAPTER FOUR

TEMPLE awoke to the buzzing of a moth behind the bamboo blinds. Sunshine was slanting into her bedroom, casting tiger stripes across the matting.

She pushed aside her bed netting and gazed around the room which she had been too tired last night to really notice. There was a carved chest lacquered gold and blue, with a mirror upon it, and a large matching wardrobe ... exquisite lacquering, shimmering like butterfly wings. Her bed had tall posts to hold the tropical netting, and cut boldly in the teakwood were carvings of tigers with gilded eyes, foliage and birds – symbols, she realized, of strength, fertility, and happiness.

The walls of the room were a cool ivory, and there were low chairs of bamboo, and a bamboo bed-table with a blue-shaded lamp upon it.

Even as she gazed round fascinated, the split-bamboo curtain that screened her room made a chik-chak sound and Mei entered carrying a tray on which stood a glass of fruit juice.

The ivory-skinned girl wore a cheongsam this morning, its high collar giving her dignity in contrast to Temple's tousled figure in the big painted bed. 'You sleep good, *mem*?' Mei handed her the glass of fruit juice. 'I cook eggs for *mem* to eat on vlanda.'

'I shall enjoy that.' Temple found the juice tart and cool, and as she sipped it she tried to read friendliness in the tilting dark eyes of Mei Flower. The girl gazed back at her with an unreadable expression, and Temple wondered if she felt resentful. The teahouse had been hers to use as a home, and now she had a mistress to serve!

'You take bath, *mem*?'

41

'Is there such a thing in the house?' Temple asked eagerly.

'Teahouse got bath, no taps, but Mei pour water.'

Temple smiled, and then flushed slightly as a faint gleam of contempt came into Mei's eyes as she turned to the lacquered wardrobe and opened it. She surveyed the few dresses inside, and then gave Temple a bland, inquiring look.

'The blue one.' Temple set aside the glass she had emptied and slipped from her bed. Her Chinese pyjamas were crumpled, and suddenly she wanted more than anything to be bathed and neatly clad in the blue home-spun which she had bought at Lumbaya. She wanted to feel cool and composed and not set at a disadvantage by the other girl, who had not a hair of her smooth dark head out of place.

The bathhouse was at the rear of the teahouse, not exactly the height of luxury with its great teakwood tub, but once the tepid water had been tilted in from the big water jars, Temple was happy to splash about and wash herself with the last of her lanolin bar of soap. There must, she thought, be a store on the island where she would be able to buy soap and toothpaste and a few other adjuncts to civilized living.

She emerged from the bathhouse feeling fresh and eager to begin her first day's work on the island. Clad in a bathrobe and letting her hair dry in the sunshine, she gazed around the compound at the silky casuarina trees, and the flowering cloves and camphors. Small birds fluttered among them, gaudy as flowers, and a great cluster of frangipani hung its bells over a corner of the pagoda-eaved veranda.

Cicadas purred harshly, hidden among the green and the flame. A chameleon hopped across Temple's foot and she started back in alarm as Mei came out on the veranda and gazed at her with that faint insolence veiled by a bland politeness.

'You have *makan* now?' she asked.

'When I have dressed.' Temple hurried indoors to her room and felt the quick beating of her pulse. She had not imagined that Mei was resentful of her, and as she smoothed the blue homespun down over her slender hips she wondered if the girl thought of her in the light of a rival.

Nick had not been averse to the charms of an island girl, and as Temple brushed her hair she saw the sudden pain in her eyes which the mirror reflected. Ryk van Helden was unmarried and alone, and last night on the veranda he had remarked that Mei was like a flower.

Temple slipped her mother's ring upon her finger and felt a little less alone. She studied her reflection and thought without vanity that the blue dress looked cool and attractive. She was very much a girl again after two days of masquerading as a boy – not that Mijnheer van Helden had been fooled! She turned hastily from the mirror to avoid seeing the colour that came into her cheeks.

Her breakfast of small fried eggs, *broodjes* and butter had been laid on a cane table near the cluster of pale frangipani. There was a china pot of the most delicious tea Temple had ever tasted, and Mei pointed a hand towards the green heart of the island. 'From the *tuanku's* tea valley,' she lisped, her eyes demure behind silky lashes.

Temple poured a second cup of the golden brew, and was in no doubt to whom Mei referred. Master ... owner ... Ryk van Helden.

Mei slipped silently away, and Temple finished her breakfast in a thoughtful mood. The sunlight filled the compound, reflecting the pagoda shadow of the teahouse with its curving roof. The wind-bells were silent, nothing stirred but the scent of the frangipani. Temple put out a hand to touch the cluster, and as she did so something

43

dark stirred among the white flowers and scampered upon her arm before she could draw back.

'Ugh!' She leapt to her feet and brushed wildly at the object. It fell to the ground and in an instant had scuttled into hiding behind the cool white cloak of temple-flower ... a crook-legged spider covered in dark hair.

Temple backed to the veranda rail, then suddenly she ran down the steps and across the compound, still brushing at her arm, still feeling the tickle of those eight legs. It could, she knew, have been venomous, but she had brushed it off too quickly to have acquired a bite.

She hurried along the shady *laan* that led to the palace, and tried not to believe that Mei had placed her breakfast table beside the frangipani because she knew a spider nested there. Tiny things had clung to the rotund body; a mass of baby spiders.

Temple was not the nervous, silly sort, but the incident had shaken her. All the way to the palace she could feel things crawling on her dress, and was glad to enter the orderly *sala* with its gleaming furniture and clean aroma of polish and clove tobacco.

She sat down at the desk to catch her breath, and noticed that Polyana's first diary had been placed in readiness for her. She picked up the diary and let it fall open where it would. A smile touched her lips and the sunshine grew warm again as she read what Polyana had written at breakfast on a Monday morning long ago.

'Today my dear Laurens said a thing to remember. Heaven, he said to me, is a smiling wife.'

The ceiling fan purred, and Temple sat absorbed in the diary. It was no wonder Ryk van Helden wished these revelations of his ancestress to be published in book form. The domestic passages held warmth and humanity; other pages thronged with characters and incident from the Dutch colonial past.

Polyana had been observant and blessed with a

descripive pen, and the people she wrote about and described took hold of Temple's imagination. Especially Laurens, who had combined the ruthless shrewdness of the Indies trader with a romantic heart well hidden from the rest of the world until Polyana discovered it. But not right away! She wrote that upon meeting her husband for the first time she expected a kiss and received instead a cool bow from the waist.

'Welcome, *Mevrow*,' he said, as if to a guest. 'I hope the Indies will please you, and that you will find my house comfortable.'

'Here I was in the Indies,' wrote Polyana, 'far from Holland, far from England, where I had lived as a child. I was a bride, a wife, and so unnerved by Laurens – far taller than any other man I had ever seen, with eyes that changed from dark to light grey, holding a tinge of clearest blue. Laurens, my husband, who commanded the people of a large island and a fleet of merchant ships, and who had married – so I thought in my girlish innocence – to have a mistress for his big house above the tea valley ...

'I was to learn differently,' Polyana wrote. 'And it was a lesson that held tears before I found myself no longer a pupil but a passionately happy woman.'

Temple drew forward the typewriter and placed a carbon between two sheets of manuscript paper. She inserted them and began to type the story of Polyana van Helden ... Each jewel upon the glove was an incident, a story, a pain and often a kiss ...

Never had a morning passed so swiftly and pleasurably. Temple sat back in her chair and stretched her arms, and then she arose to go and eat her lunch in the garden.

Ranji had placed the food on a small table beneath a blossom tree, and he showed his gold teeth in a smile as he bowed Temple into her seat by the lotus-pond and removed the cover from yellow slices of mango, chilled and juicy. After the mango she had baked fish and sweet potatoes, followed by creamy chunks of custard-apple.

She drank her coffee in a contented mood, and watched the pink lotus flowers floating on their velvety leaves on the water of the pond. Cicadas chirred in the sunlit trees, and she watched the monkeys at play in a great *waringin*; the banyan whose meshed and curving branches were never cut, because to cut the sacred tree was to invite bad luck. The monkeys chattered and swung among the branches, and one of the more daring hopped to the edge of the table and took a piece of fruit.

Temple returned to her work. The palace was becalmed, with not a sound to be heard but the tap-tap of her typewriter. Siesta time, when the tropical heat made people too drowsy for work. They curled beneath a net or a tree and slept, and so were ready for work in the cool of the evening.

Temple was feeling the heat herself. It penetrated into the *sala* and could not be kept at bay by the ceiling fans. Her fingers began to feel sticky on the typewriter keys and her dress clung to her body; suddenly she yawned and decided that a stroll might wake her up.

She placed a bronze Chinese horse on the chapter she had typed, drank some lime juice, and wandered out of the *sala* into the hall of the palace. It was a vista of gleaming tiles, tall lacquered columns, fretted doorways . . . antiquity and silence.

She glanced into several of the rooms and found them much like the *sala*, well-polished and rather impersonal, and when she drew near to the ornate double staircase she mounted the wide steps to the gallery shaped like a horseshoe. She began to make her way along the gallery when suddenly there was a red-gold flash and something bounded from the shadows of a doorway and wrapped its paws about her legs.

'*Oh!*' She glanced down, not knowing what to expect, and found that her assailant was a tiger-cub, a playful creature with a loud purr.

'Well, I never!' Temple loved animals and she bent down eagerly to stroke him. He thrust his round head into her hand and bit playfully at her fingers. A pet of some importance, for he wore a collar studded with tiny stones. 'Now who are you, I wonder?' Temple caressed his belly as he rolled over, paws in the air, quivering with that peculiar pleasure of animals whose instincts are never wrong about people.

Near where Temple played with the cub was the carved teakwood door of one of the upper rooms. She glanced at the door and felt the silence filled with the cub's purring, and almost of its own accord her hand reached out to try the handle of the door. She meant only to glance inside, but directly the door was open the cub bounded in and the next moment had leapt upon the bed.

'Oh, lord!' Temple raced to pluck him off the bed before he tore the threads of the silk cover. He growled in imitation of his fierce jungle parent, and Temple stood with him in her arms as she gazed around the room, caught and held by its beauty, which the filtering sunshine through the blinds revealed in a strange, haunting way.

Silk piled carpets lay upon the warm golden teak of the floor. Window drapes of golden silk hung to the floor, and an immense peacock-feather fan was spread against one of the walls. The furniture was delicately carved, and there were mirrors with a bloom over them, as though rarely were they polished and looked into.

On the dressing-table stood filigree toilet boxes and matching lamps with silk shades. The niello-backed brushes and combs stood on little lace mats ... not the possessions of a man but those of a woman ... a woman whose beauty would blend with such surroundings.

47

Suddenly the room seemed filled with something ominous. The tiger-cub leapt from Temple's arms and ran out of the door, but she could not follow. She was held as if by a ghostly hand on her shoulder; as if something in this room was inciting her to explore, to find the secret which it held.

She moved and brushed against the silk of the bedspread, honey gold, padded and soft to the touch. She opened a cupboard and found it bare. She drew open a drawer and breathed the scent of sandalwood. A beautiful room, but never used!

She met her own questing eyes in the mirror of the dressing-table; she felt as she looked, young and unsophisticated, with a willowy body and a heart that beat fast as she opened a little silver box that stood in front of her. A single jade earring lay in the silver box. Apple-green jade, carved and glimmering, and she was holding it against her earlobe to get the effect when a tall figure loomed behind her in the mirror.

The earring dropped from her hand as she swung round guiltily. Ryk van Helden bent to pick it up. He replaced it in the silver box without saying a word. His cold and chilly expression spoke for him; there was a dangerous set to his mouth.

'I – I'm sorry,' she said nervously. 'The door wasn't locked, you see—'

'That is no excuse!' His voice, his entire being was charged with a cold, whiplash anger. 'The *sala* is your province, Miss Lane. I employed you to work there, not to wander about my private rooms while I am absent from the *kraton*. Is that what you have been doing all day? Prying into things that are none of your concern?'

She flushed hotly and hated the man. Hated everything about him in that humiliating moment ... arrogant, sarcastic brute!

48

'If the woman who had this room ran out on you, then I can't say I blame her!' Temple threw at him.

An ominous silence followed, and Temple felt the frightened pounding of her heart as an angry pallor spread beneath his tan. His hands clenched beside his khaki trousers; his powerful body seemed tense with the desire to inflict violence.

'No one ever had this room, nor ever shall,' he said harshly. 'That earring you were playing about with was all that was left of the girl I was going to marry. Her name was Marta, and the plane that was bringing her from Leyden crashed in the mountains of Sumatra three years ago. I was waiting in Sumatra, where we were to be married. I went up into the mountains with the rescue team, but there was no one left to rescue. Only by the earring, only by her wheaten blonde hair was I able to identify Marta. I had sent her the earrings as a gift, and even death could not take the life from her golden hair.'

He gazed broodingly around the room which he had filled with lovely things for the girl he had loved.

Temple sagged back against the dressing-table and felt as if all the life had gone out of her own body. A little surf of sunshine rippled in and out of the room, and below in one of the courtyards a peacock cried.

'I – I had no idea,' she said. 'I thought—'

'You thought the obvious, and why not?' It was almost a jeer. 'Planters and timber men take mistresses to alleviate their loneliness, like your boy-friend back in Lumbaya.'

'Don't, please!' Tears came into her eyes.

'Provoke and expect to be bitten.' An expression of tiredness crept over his face, deepening the lines in it, a contrast to the tousled, vibrant hair. 'You were bound to see this room, and I suppose it angered me to come upon you here—' His lips twisted, cynically. 'I have lived too long in the Indies not to make my shrine ... what

49

do you think of it?'

'It's a very beautiful room.' Temple felt his pain, and another that had a sharp edge to it. This room had been meant for a girl with wheaten blonde hair – a beautiful Dutch girl from Leyden – and he could not bear another girl to come in here and touch these things. She looked at him, and thought of Nick, and knew that nothing like this had touched her heart. The passion, and the torment of irreparable loss.

'I knew Marta when I was a boy of sixteen and she a small girl of eight with long fair plaits. Her parents were neighbours of my *grootmoeder* at Leyden, where we lived in an old castle. Marta loved to come and play in the castle – captive princess, you know.' He smiled briefly, and for a fleeting moment Temple glimpsed a tenderness in this tall, hard tiger of a man.

He began to pace back and forth, hands thrust into the pockets of his khaki trousers, and then he paused beside the bed and his work-hardened hand rasped against the silk as he touched it. 'Chinese – the silk in which a concubine was wrapped and carried to the apartment of her master. Marta loved such stories. She was a great dreamer—'

He sighed harshly, and glanced across at Temple. 'Come, I will show you the rest of the palace. Perhaps you would like to go to the rooftop? From there one has a view of the volcano, and of the village and the tea valley. Come!'

They left Marta's room, and the tiger-cub padded along behind them as they made their way up a flight of stairs that led to the terrace surrounding the pagoda roof of the palace.

Temple caught her breath, both at the view, and at the large hand that caught her by the waist as she went near the edge of the terrace. The volcano stood disembodied from the mountains, its cone blue-tinted and edged by the gold of the declining sun. The tea valley was a deep pocket of green, hung round by tier upon tier of gleaming rice *padi.*

'I had no idea the island was so large, *meneer.*' There was a husky catch in Temple's voice, and she was acutely aware of the man at her side; of the strong brown hands that could have locked themselves about her narrow waist. Below the palace the thatched houses of the village stood on stilts among the flame trees. The trees rustled and it was as though they breathed.

'We will wait and watch the sun go down.' He lifted the cub, which settled about his shoulders like a muff of red-gold, blinking green eyes in petted contentment. 'A gift from Prince Chai,' Ryk said dryly. 'I call him Kitpup, because he's a combination of puppy antics and kitten-ish wiles.'

Temple smiled as the cub nuzzled his master's throat. It seemed appropriate that Ryk should be rearing a tiger for a pet.

'Dig in my pocket,' he said suddenly. 'I found some lotus cones on the way home.'

They were in a pocket of his cotton bush shirt, which when peeled revealed a nest of tasty little nuts. She and Ryk stood chewing them, and she tried to forget that only a short while ago he had lashed out at her ... had looked her up and down as though it were a cruel jest that she should be here in place of Marta.

'Does the volcano ever erupt?' she asked.

'Now and then it grumbles. The islanders say that when the gods are angry with someone on the island, then they speak through the volcano and it shakes the earth in warning.'

'Then I hope while I am here that the islanders don't anger the gods.' She smiled, but her eyes were pensive as they dwelt on the sky surrounding the great cone. The sun had gone to topaz, the west was aflame, tinged with a deep violet. Again a peacock cried, and the air was charged with something elemental.

In a breathless silence she stood beside Ryk and watched the tropical dusk steal over Bayanura. Surely never again would she see and feel such magic. She sighed and felt a wonderful coolness steal over her.

'I have seen other sunsets, but on Bayanura they have a special beauty of their own.' Ryk's voice was deeptoned in the dusk, and Temple sensed the trend of his thoughts. Such sunsets would he have shared with Marta, and in the tropical dusk he would have turned to her and taken her in his arms. His captive princess, come to share with him a palace on a peacock island.

'Come!' A harsh word of command for Temple Lane, and she followed him in silence, too unaccustomed to tenderness to expect it from Ryk van Helden.

They made their way down to the *sala*, where he inspected her day's work while Ranji brought them sundowners. Long drinks in which pieces of ice bobbed, Ryk stretched in a rattan long chair while Temple stood in the fretted archway and sipped her drink. The scent of the flowers was stronger in the dusk, dark passionate blooms with deep, secretive hearts. Long leaves like whispering tongues, the chirrup of gecko, the fluttering shadow of a large moth.

'You are an excellent typist.' Ryk had lit a cigarette and the clove-tinged smoke floated over to her. 'I hope you found the work interesting?'

'Did you think I found it tiresome, *meneer*, because I—' Her hands clenched about the long glass holding her drink. 'I felt warm, my hands were sticky on the keys—'

'Forget it.'

'Very well.' She turned her gaze to the garden once more, but she would not forget quickly that encounter in the beautiful room planned for his bride. She would remember each detail ... the cool golden colours, the jade earring, the Chinese silk in which long ago a concubine had been carried to her master.

When Ryk was alone here, did he wander into that room, his heart eaten up by a dream that had made him discard all other dreams?

He did not ask her to stay and share his rice-table. Bayu, one of his house boys, saw her home to the tea-house.

CHAPTER FIVE

As the days passed, Temple began to settle down to her task of typing the diaries and living on a tropical island.

The day would start with the golden sun rising out of the tea valley, and after breakfast on the veranda – at some distance from the frangipani – Temple would make her way to the palace. Ryk seemed to start work at the crack of dawn, and then she learned from Ranji that the *tuan* went for a swim each morning.

Temple thought of Mei, her dark hair glossy with water each morning as she served breakfast, a glow about her skin, a secret look in her eyes. She swam as well, Temple realized, and from then on she tried to keep her attitude towards Ryk as impersonal as possible. She was here to work, not to join him in activities outside the realms of employment.

It was on Friday afternoon that Temple heard a small aeroplane circling the island. She had finished her day's stint and was up on the terrace as the plane began to glide in for a landing at the other side of the village, where a runway was kept clear for the Prince, and for the island's 'flying doctor'.

Temple shaded her eyes with her hand and watched the plane disappear below the waving palms and clustering bamboos; the sound of the engine died away and Temple felt a stirring of curiosity. Ryk had said that Dr. Kinraid flew to the island about once a week, and she was bound to meet him.

What would be his reaction at finding an English girl on the Dutchman's island?

A little later Temple slipped away without waiting for Ryk to appear for his sundowner and his usual few words about the progress of the manuscript. She left the work ready for him to check and made her way to the beach, carrying the bathing sarong and towel which she had brought to the palace that morning.

She would swim alone in the cool of the evening and not intrude on Ryk, whose attitude made it plain that when the working day was over she might as well be a piece of office equipment.

She found the beach, glimmering white until it was lost in the dusk. Fishing boats put in at the other side of the island where there were less rocks, which left this part of the shore isolated and exactly suited to Temple's solitary mood. She stripped off in one of the caves and donned the sarong. The palm trees rustled and the breeze was cool on her limbs as she ran down into the surf.

It lapped and curled around her legs, lifted her and carried her out on small buoyant waves. It was a pagan feeling to swim in a sarong, alone in the silky darkness of the sea, with only the golden gaze of the stars upon her. Such giant stars in a sky of purple, making her aware of how far away she was from familiar things.

Her thoughts turned to Nick and she wondered what his reaction had been when he had found her gone. Did he miss her and wonder where she might be? Or had he already forgotten her in the arms of Lua?

The waves were racing and swelling beneath her, and it helped to dull the sudden pain to fight with them. This pain must mean that she cared still for Nick, or that she clung to the dream she had lived with for five years. A broken dream went on hurting ... even a man as strong and hard as Ryk van Helden was not invulnerable when it came to dreams. His had been destroyed in the highlands of Sumatra. The tiger land, from which he had returned a different man from the one known to Marta, the girl from Leyden with the long flaxen hair.

It was then that a gasp escaped from Temple. Her

sarong had become unwrapped in the water and had drifted away, leaving her as nude as a naiad. She began to swim hastily towards the shore. Thank goodness she was alone and could make a quick dart among the palm trees to the cave where she had left her clothes.

She reached the shallows and was about to rise and tread water when a tall figure emerged from among the palms and stood outlined in a white shirt against the trunks of the trees.

To say that Temple was disconcerted would be putting it mildly. Even by starlight she could recognize the height and breadth of her employer. The end of his cigarette glowed and then darkened, and that keen eye of his had spotted her . . . or at least had spotted someone in the water.

'Mei, is it you?' He began to walk down the beach, and Temple kept herself hidden in the water, biting her lip in embarrassment, and something close to anger. Mei was on his mind, evidently. Mei, the little golden girl!

'Mei?' he said again.

'It's me,' Temple snapped.

'Miss Lane!' A drawl came into his voice. 'Please, don't let me stop you from coming out of the water.'

'I'm afraid you are stopping me.' She could not for the life of her make a dash out of the water with Ryk van Helden looking on.

'Really, young lady, how am I stopping you?'

'Just by being here. Please, *meneer*, do you mind going away again?'

'*Ja*, I mind.' Sand crunched beneath his tread and the surf creamed over his sandals and the bottoms of his trousers. 'Come now, I give you a hand out of the water—'

'You will not!' She swam out of reach. 'I – I've lost my sarong – and can't possibly come out of the water with you standing there.'

56

'But, *meisje*,' he was laughing, 'how can you be embarrassed with *me*? Remember the steamer?'

'Yes, I remember!' Temple was quite sure she hated him. He was so mocking, and it was always other people who seemed to be at his mercy. 'Please go away and stop bedevilling me.'

'Is that what I am doing?' He was still chuckling, his cigarette in a corner of his mouth, as he turned his back and stripped off his shirt. 'Come out and slip into this,' he ordered.

She hesitated, and then hurriedly obeyed him, a wet, white figure in the starlight as she grabbed the shirt, warm from his body, and slipped it over her head. It enveloped her to her thighs, and as she fastened the buttons her cheeks burned. 'W-what a fool you must think me,' she muttered.

'You have it on?'

'Yes.' The cuffs hung down over her hands and her slim body was concealed, all but her slender legs.

Ryk turned to look at her, the smoke of his cigarette drifting from his lips. 'If ever you need another job, then you must become a model for the *mannetje* look,' he teased. 'There is something – is it alchemy? – about a girl dressed in a masculine shirt.'

Temple backed away from him, instinctively. The stars glimmered in the sea and the sea-light was reflected on to the beach, and she caught the ripple of chest muscle as Ryk lounged back against a palm tree. Something leapt and crackled in the air between them, and she said with a shiver that she was cold and would go and put on her clothes in the cave.

She ran from him, unashamedly, and in the dimness of the cave she listened to the churning of the sea and visualized him by the palm tree as she took a quick rub down and slipped into her clothes. She picked up his shirt, to which clung the aroma of clove tobacco, and

57

wondered why there was none of the ease of friendship between them. He mocked whenever he came to her rescue. He was cool and crisp when he came to the *sala* to discuss the diaries with her.

She pressed his shirt between her hands, but the material did not wrinkle. It was fine, even faintly silky . . . like the skin of a girl with secret, slanting eyes.

Temple rejoined him and handed him the shirt. He drew it down over his head and his wide shoulders, and left it unbuttoned at his throat. 'I thought you had gone back to the teahouse,' he said. 'Instead you felt like a swim, *ja*?'

'*Ja*.' She felt a little more composed, and could even smile as she recalled her panic when he had emerged from among the trees. 'I made myself a sarong, but the darn thing came undone in the water. One of the mishaps I seem prone to since I left my safe little job in England.'

'Safe, what is that?' He snapped his fingers. 'A week ago you were the champion of your own absurdities . . . is it so shocking a thing for an English girl to lose her bathing dress?'

'You seem to think it a great joke,' she said frigidly. 'And I do agree that it's a predicament an island girl like Mei would be unlikely to get into – unless she wished to.'

'What if I assumed that you wished to be alluring?' he drawled. 'The stars shine among the palms, the sea whispers, and we are quite alone . . . two people who have loved and lost.'

'It would be empty consolation, *meneer*, even if I thought for one minute that you were serious—'

'What makes you so sure, *meisje*, that I am not serious?'

'I am an efficient typist, *meneer*, a piece of office equipment. You wouldn't dream of embracing a filing cabinet!'

He laughed, and as Temple listened to his laughter she

58

kicked at the shingle. The swell of the waves and the white rim of foam about the rocks made them stand out with the cruel clarity of his mockery. 'I heard a plane arrive,' she said. 'Was it Dr. Kinraid?'

'Yes, it was *de vliegende dokter*.' Still that note of mockery threaded his words. 'You must meet him, Miss Lane. He dines with me tonight and you must join us.'

'I should have to change into something a little more formal.'

'As you wish.' He said it as if Dr. Kinraid would not be impressed one way or the other and without speaking they made their way through the trees to the teahouse. The thin bamboo blinds at the windows were like shadow screens, and the slim figure of Mei could be seen moving about in the lounge as Ryk paused beside Temple at the little gate of the compound.

As he opened the gate, his gaze dwelt on the shadow that flitted back and forth with the slender grace of a mantis. 'Have you made friends with Mei?' he asked.

'She is quiet and efficient,' Temple replied, and the evening breeze rustled the frangipani to remind her that the girl was not entirely to be trusted.

'You speak with a certain reservation.' His gaze sharpened upon Temple. 'Does she remind you of that other girl – the one at Lumbaya?'

'I suppose she does.'

'To you these girls are like almonds peeled from the same shell, *ja*?' He pushed open the gate and Temple slipped through to the compound. The clove trees rustled and their blossoms burned darkly and spiced the air with a musky, throat-catching scent. Temple looked at Ryk, for whom the flower face of Mei held no secrets – dark secrets, things known that could entice a man from the straight path into the jungle. *Nick*. His name arose like a sob in her throat, and she said huskily:

'Don't wait for me, *meneer*. I'll join you at the palace.'

59

'You will not be nervous of coming alone?'

'No. I'm getting used to the island at night.' She smiled, a twist of the lips and the heart. She had to learn to be alone for longer than it took to walk the *laan* to the palace.

'Mei has told me about the ghost,' she added, forcing a laugh. 'The *yogini*, or princess, who used to slip away from the palace to meet her lover under the clove-trees of the teahouse.'

'But the English are not afraid of ghosts, only of minor embarrassments.' A quizzing, piratical look, intensified by the eye-patch. 'I will see you at the palace, *ja'wel*?'

'Yes. I have not changed my mind about wanting to meet the flying doctor.'

'It is romantic, you think, to be a doctor who flies from island to island to care for the sick?'

'Very romantic,' she agreed, a tilt to her chin. 'Is Dr. Kinraid a young man?'

'He has about the same number of years as myself.' Something not entirely humorous pulled at Ryk's lips. 'But you will think him younger – a decade younger than I. Perhaps because he is an American. Perhaps for other reasons.' A cool bow of courtesy and then Ryk was gone, among the trees and their shadows.

Temple stood gazing after him, a man whose youth had died in him three years ago when he had gone into the mountains of Sumatra and returned with a single earring of Han jade. Temple felt chilled and she hurried into the teahouse, where she told Mei not to bother about supper because she would be dining at the palace.

Mei gazed at her with inscrutable eyes, taking in her sea-tangled hair and the wrinkles in her cotton shirt and trews. 'The *tuanku* invite you to eat alone with him?' she asked, her voice as expressionless as her eyes.

'Of course not.' Temple wondered coldly why she bothered to explain herself to the girl. 'Dr. Kinraid has arrived for the weekend and Mijnheer van Helden wishes me to meet him.'

Mei's silky dark lashes swept down over her eyes. 'The *nonya* wishes me to help her dress?'

'No, I can manage.' Temple felt the veiled gaze as she turned and went through the *chik* into the corridor that led to her room. She entered her room and put on the lamp, and as she combed the tangles out of her hair she smelled the sea and the wind in the short dark strands. Ryk always seemed to come along at the most awkward moments, and she had to do something to restore a little of her lost dignity. She turned to the wardrobe and opened it, and after a hesitant moment she took out the white sheath with an embroidered hem which she had bought to please Nick and which she had not yet worn. It was of heavy shantung and sleeveless, and the embroidery was striking.

Yes, she would wear it tonight, and then as she stroked the silk she noticed that her garnet ring was missing from her hand. She wore it day and night, and the only time she had left it off was on board the steamer when she had posed as a youth. Her mother's ring! Which she had certainly been wearing when she had covered the typewriter after finishing work for the day. She remembered knocking the ring sideways on her finger and straightening it with a fond smile. It was not all that valuable in a material sense, but it meant a lot to her.

She must have lost it down on the shore. In the cave – or in the water. Tomorrow she would go down and search for it, but right now she had to get dressed for supper at the palace.

She looked lissom and at the same time very feminine in the white shantung. Her evening sandals had slender heels that increased her height, and lacking a stole she draped a chiffon scarf about her shoulders. Her dark hair, with its peak in the centre of her forehead, gave the

61

effect of a medieval cap, and her young neck rose slenderly from the slight V of her dress.

Mei was not in the lounge as Temple made her way out of the teahouse, but when she reached the gate of the compound and glanced back she saw a still and silent figure at the end of the veranda. The wind-bells tinkled and though Temple knew that it was only a breeze that touched her bare arms under the chiffon of her scarf, it felt like cold fingers.

The spark flies were alight in the dark, and Temple used her small hand torch to light her way along the *laan*. The air was heavy with the scent of the trailing lianas, and in the jungle of banyans and wild pepper trees, the great fronds of fern, and the flame trees quenched in the dark, there was a persistent sound of tokay, tokay.

Tokay . . . until something cracked behind her in the underbrush and all her nerves seemed to tighten for a moment. She swung the torch and lit the dark, clustering foliage . . . and again that stealthy tread broke a twig. Temple caught her breath. Here in the close scented darkness she was alone with something that crept through the trees, that stirred a thicket, that breathed a cold hostility down the back of her slim neck . . .

She caught at the long skirt of her dress and began to run, and she did not pause until she reached the court-yard of the palace. The hanging lanterns in the fretted arcades cast pools of light, and the fountain splashed as she leaned against a wall and regained her breath. She didn't want to enter the palace in an agitated state, and was slightly ashamed now of having given way to her nerves.

Ryk van Helden would be especially amused, and she would not give him the satisfaction of a drawling inquiry as to whom she thought had frightened her – the *yogini*, on her way to keep a ghostly tryst?

Temple smoothed her dress and her hair and dropped

her torch into her purse. In her flight she had lost her chiffon scarf, but that couldn't be helped, and chin tilted, she entered the palace through an archway and crossed the old and lovely tiles of the hall to the open teakwood door of the *salon*, from out of which came the sound of male voices. One of the men laughed ... it was not Ryk.

Temple paused unnoticed in the doorway and stood looking in at Ryk and his guest. Both men wore white dinner jackets over dark trousers. Both men were in the prime of condition, with that burned-in bronze look that was extra startling against the white jackets. Tough, able, and as much a part of these islands as the sun and the ocean wind and the volcanic mountains.

Suddenly Ryk noticed her and she tensed as his keen grey eye flicked her from head to foot. Dr. Kinraid followed his glance and studied the slender girl framed by the teakwood which was inset with mother-of-pearl. He smiled, his blue eyes etched by lines of humour and tolerance.

'This is Temple Lane,' said Ryk. 'This is the young waif from out of nowhere. Temple, meet Alan Kinraid.'

The doctor held out a brown, lean-fingered hand and Temple shook it. 'I'm very glad to know you, Dr. Kinraid. I've heard of flying doctors and the wonderful work they do, but this is the first time I have met one.'

'This is the first time I've met a waif who turns out to be a charming young woman.' His blue eyes took in her cap of dark hair with its peak, and Temple was aware that Ryk watched her meeting with his friend with a sardonic air about him

'Will you have a drink before we go into supper?' he asked.

'A small sherry, please.' She was still a little shaky, and a drink would help to dispel the feeling. Alan Kinraid watched, with perhaps a professional glint in his eyes, as she drank her sherry.

'Are you getting involved with Polyana and her adventures?' he asked. 'Ryk has been good enough to let me read one or two of the diaries and they are certainly worthy of publication.'

'I'm enjoying the work immensely. Polyana is so alive, and she brings to life all the people she knew and loved.' Temple smiled shyly. 'Women are going to love the book when it's published – I think it should be serialized and I've suggested to *meneer* that he write to the publishers and sound them out.'

'Ryk, this is a most efficient young waif.' Alan shot him a look which held a gleam of curiosity. 'I hope you appreciate her, and don't overwork her.'

'I am aware, Alan, that the Dutch planters owned slaves in the old days,' Ryk said drily, 'but Miss Lane is English and would never submit to being enslaved.'

'I should hope, *meneer*,' she said, 'that the days are long over when men expected women to bow down to their every command.'

'You are now in the Indies,' he drawled, 'where the women are still great charmers because they have not forgotten that without the male palm there are no coconuts, and no datura blossom without the pollen.'

'You like women to be dependent upon men?'

'Men and women are dependent upon each other.'

'But you prefer the woman who reaches to a man's shoulder rather than the one who goes above his head?'

'Ryk has lived too long in the East to appreciate the changes that are taking place in Europe and America.' Alan smiled, somewhat wryly. 'And perhaps I stay here myself because the women of my country depend these days more on intellect than instinct. They direct their own emotions without letting their emotions direct them.'

'A woman should be like the bamboo, flexible, grace-

ful, and strong even though she looks fragile.' Ryk bowed
sardonically at Temple. 'So say the islanders, and I am
inclined to agree with their slant on life.'

'You must visit my bamboo hospital in the village,'
said Alan to Temple. 'It's small, but we're quite proud of
it ... do you know, Ryk, if you hadn't snapped up
Temple for your secretary, I should have asked her to
work for me.'

'Miss Lane will be free to work for whoever she chooses,
when her work on the diaries is completed.' There was a
slightly arrogant ring in his voice, echoed by the boom
of a gong in the hall. A manservant appeared in the doorway of the *salon*, clad in a robe and a dark velvet cap.

'Come,' said Ryk, 'our supper is ready.'

Alan offered his arm to Temple, and she felt his
fingers close briefly over hers. As they crossed the hall
they passed the bronze statue of Kwan Yin. 'The goddess,'
said Alan, 'who let heaven wait while she gave comfort
to a crying child.'

'And that,' smiled Temple, 'is the perfect definition
of the true woman.'

'But she should not,' he murmured, 'let heaven wait
too long.'

CHAPTER SIX

THE room in which they dined – high table to the Dutch, who liked to dine late – was ornately decorative. The furniture was of black and gold lacquer, and great curtains draped the windows, embroidered with the peacock and the lotus. The round table was lit by candles in bronze stands, and golden-bird orchids were clustered in a silver bowl at the centre of the table.

'Lovely strange flowers!' Temple touched them and poked a finger into the velvety 'beak' of one of them.

'Flowers that hide their hearts are always exciting – like women who do the same.' Alan was looking at Temple as he spoke, but she kept her gaze on her bowl of turtle soup. It was easy for a man to be flirtatious when he knew he was going away again, and Temple no longer trusted in charm since Nick had let her down.

'This soup is delicious, *meneer*,' she said.

'If you are here when the islanders hold their Feast of the Moon, then you will see the men bringing in the turtles for the feast.' The candlelight was illusory and made Ryk look gentler. 'They rope them in the water and ride them as a cowboy would a steer.'

'Strange how large they grow when a baby turtle can be held in the palm of the hand.' Alan looked keen and humorous. 'Nature is an awesome thing.'

'Even to a doctor?' Temple smiled.

'Alan is a boy at heart,' drawled Ryk, 'that is why he prefers to be a flying doctor rather than a dignified consultant in a glass office. He has all the qualifications, Miss Lane.'

'Bar the inclination.' Alan quirked an eyebrow at Ryk, as if the Dutchman's formality amused him. 'Could you give up your island for an office in Amsterdam?'

'*Dit is mijn huis*,' Ryk growled. 'Each one of us carries the past in his blood, and it is here I have my roots. Roots that bled during my years in Leyden – if I could have lived there—' Harsh memory deepened the lines in his face, and he sat silent as their second course was brought, along with a bottle of wine which Ranji wiped on a snowy napkin, leaving a rim of cellar dust on the napkin. He poured a little into a stemmed glass and Ryk tasted it. '*Ja*.' He nodded, the blind side of his face to Temple as she glanced at him. If he could have lived at Leyden, then Marta would still be alive. She would not have been killed in the tiger land!

The wine was old and warm-coloured, and with it was served baked lobster, and rice roasted in cylinders of bamboo, so that when the bamboo was peeled the rice emerged crisply flavoured.

'*Smakelijk!*' Alan ate his bamboo rice-sticks with boyish enjoyment. 'What do you think of this Dutch-Asian food, Temple?'

'I like the inventive ways in which the islanders cook their rice. To eat it like this is certainly a change from the stolid rice puddings my aunt used to cook.' Her hazel eyes caught the candlelight as she took a sip of wine, and she smiled inwardly as she thought of her cousins and what they would say if they could see their orphan cousin right now. It was slightly unreal to herself that she sat dining with the *tuan besar* of an island in the Indies, and a blue-eyed doctor who piloted a plane to visit his patients

'I wonder what Temple is thinking when she smiles like that?' There was a gleam of whimsical humour in Alan's eyes as he studied her. 'Women are the most mysterious of creatures ... even to a doctor!'

'I imagine that Miss Lane is thinking of the beckoning hand of the unknown, which a woman always has to follow ... even in trepidation.' It was Ryk who spoke, and the deep tone of his voice seemed to add a note of significance to what he said. She thought of their encounter down on the beach ... she didn't really know him at all, yet here she was, a guest at his table. She did fear him; or something within him that prowled restlessly, seeking the peace and the promise he had lost with the loss of Marta.

She lowered her glance and was glad when the conversation between the two men veered to island matters she had no part in. She listened to the deep accented tones mingling with the whimsical American voice, and wondered why the doctor was still unattached. Perhaps his work kept him single, for though he had his home base at Bang-palem, he was kept busy flying from island to island.

Ranji, solemn in his robe and black velvet cap, prepared for them a dessert which Temple had never tasted. She watched its preparation with enchanted eyes, only half aware of the two men who watched her. Alan leaned forward. 'You child,' he laughed in a low tone. Ryk looked sardonic in the candlelight as he twirled the stem of his wine glass between his fingers.

'Watch, *nonya*.' Ranji flashed his golden smile at Temple, and the next moment blue flames lit the table as he ignited the brandy over the papaya and cream, then with a deft hand he served the dessert while it was still aflame.

'It's like a Christmas party!' Temple caught Ryk's eye, and then in confusion she glanced down at her plate. She felt the quick beating of a pulse in her throat, and she knew that he thought her as unawakened as a child. Nick Hallam had not touched the springs of her being. Knowing him had no more than opened her eyes to the disillusion a girl can encounter when she sets out in the world.

They returned to the *salon* to drink their coffee. The tiger-cub was sprawled on one of the Indian rugs, and his purring kept time with the soft whirring of the antique fans. The plaintive music of a bamboo flute stole in from the heart of the garden.

'What will you do with that chap when he gets big enough to snarl?' Alan gestured at the cub, who lifted a lazy head to blink green eyes at him.

'I am hoping that he will remain tame.' Ryk stood lighting a cigar, and the rise and fall of the flame played over the strong contours of his face.

Alan took a puff at his cigarette – he had shaken his head at the dark cigars. 'Can you tame a tiger?' he drawled, and from her cushioned rattan chair Temple watched the doctor's blue eyes flick the lithe frame of the Dutchman, as if he too was conscious of the tiger in the man.

Ryk lowered his long body into a chair of ample proportions, and as he stretched out his legs the cub shifted his position so that his golden body lay across the man's ankles. 'I am fond of the animal, so I shall have to take a chance on his jungle instincts. Even with people,' smoke veiled the sun-lined face, 'one has to take a chance on being turned upon. One is never entirely sure of what lies behind a smile; and the prettiest teeth have been known to bite.'

'That's life,' Alan laughed. 'I like to feel a little uncertain of people rather than sure of how they'll react on every occasion. Life is drama, not a play, with set dialogue and prescribed emotions.'

'Then you don't believe in destiny?' Ryk quirked a flaxen eyebrow at Alan. 'You live and work in the East, and yet you continue to think and feel like an American – a man with his eye on the future rather than on the past?'

'No one can live in the past, Ryk.' Alan shifted in his

seat and a slight frown replaced his smile. 'The past gives us works of art and implants certain predilections in our blood, but no one walks backward, or wakes up yesterday rather than tomorrow. Tomorrow is our hope, Ryk; yesterday often a regret, and to harbour regrets makes for loneliness of spirit.'

' "Loneliness becomes a lover, solitude a darling sin." ' Ryk flicked ash into the ashtray on the teakwood table beside his chair. 'You restless Americans never could appreciate solitude.'

'If you mean I couldn't live in an old palace filled with echoes, then you're darned right.' Alan's smile was back in his eyes as he glanced at Temple. 'What do you think of Ryk's museum?' he asked.

She glanced around the *salon* with its golden birds and blue butterflies set in the panels of the glossy cabinets, its framed etchings of Eastern water scenes, and silk mats that glimmered like jewels against the teakwood floor.

'I am a newcomer to the island, so everything has significance for me, and a certain beauty.' She was aware as she spoke of Ryk in that great Dutch chair, of the sprawled tiger-cub, and a large moth buzzing around the globe of a lamp.

I never knew anything like this in my suburban home, she wanted to say. I never knew that peace could walk the night, and that violence could creep behind it like a shadow. Violence of sea and mountain, and of memory that makes a man live in loneliness with a dream. I had dreams, but they were without passion, and engendered by being unloved by those I lived with. . . .

She said none of this. She was too shy, too unsure, too aware of the passion that still brooded in Ryk van Helden. He would look cynical and smile at her youthful fancies.

'I have been here a week, but I have not yet glimpsed the peacocks,' she said. 'I hear them at dusk, and yesterday I found a tail-feather brushed with gold.'

'When they are courting they hide,' said Ryk. 'I know where they hide and you must remind me to show you their courting dance. Never is the male so proud and handsome than when he struts for the benefit of his chosen peahen.'

'It was unkind of nature to make the peahen so plain in comparison to her lord and master.' Alan lay back lazily in his rattan chair, and Temple felt him looking at her. A faint smile touched her lips. She had grown up beside a pair of flamboyant cousins and harboured few illusions about her own charms. Perhaps it was in gratitude at being noticed that she had clung to her illusions about Nick.

'I sometimes think that quiet females have more of the seductress in them than the ones who sparkle.' Alan spoke thoughtfully, and his glance brushed the pale skin of Temple's neck and arms, and drifted down her slender body in the shantung sheath with its embroidered hem. She tensed as she felt the current of his thoughts. Ryk had brought her to Bayanura . . . what did Ryk think of her as a woman?

She rose to her feet. 'It's late, *meneer*. I shall oversleep in the morning and be late for work.'

Alan laughed as he uncoiled out of his long chair. 'So speaks the eternal British secretary, efficient to her fingertips and loyal to the last semi-colon. I'll see you home through the woods, Temple!'

She hesitated, and thought of the rustlings that had followed her here. 'Thank you, Doctor.'

He had marked her hesitation and it seemed to amuse him. Ryk lifted the cub from his ankles and got to his feet. The look he flicked over Temple's bare neck and arms was sea-cool. 'I trust you have a wrap?' he said. 'Our night air is cool when the temperature drops.'

'I—' She bit her lip and could not mention that some-

71

thing had frightened her earlier on and that she had lost her scarf as she had run out of the woods in panic. 'It was warm earlier on, *meneer*—'

'And you did not think to wear a wrap. Women, *ja*?' He glanced at Alan and shrugged his wide shoulders. 'Wait a moment, Miss Lane.'

He strode out of the *salon*, leaving Temple to gaze after him in a slightly startled way. 'Strange fellow,' said Alan. 'Still very much the self-contained Dutchman despite his years in the Indies. Do you enjoy working for him?'

'I'm enjoying my work.' She had evaded a direct answer, and felt at once the keen dart of Alan's glance. 'Mijnheer is away from the palace most of the day and I'm more or less my own boss.'

'More or less,' Alan drawled. 'Ryk is a hard fellow to know, but that is on account of some of the hardships he has been through. He was here as a boy when the Japanese invaded – then during the rebellion that followed the war—' Alan took hold of a jade dragon and there was a sudden sombreness about his face. 'Ryk's mother died at that time. The old Dutch plantation house in which they were living was burned down. Mevrouw van Helden was trapped upstairs. Ryk, a mere boy, tried to get to her and was badly burned. When they got him to Leyden, a plastic surgeon operated on him, but he couldn't save the left eye ... that's how come he wears the piratical eye-patch.'

Temple's heart contracted for the boy who had fought to get to his mother through the flames of their burning house ... three times the tiger land had taken those he loved, and yet he lived here, as if under a spell that held him despite his terrible memories.

'You're wondering how he can live here?' Alan asked. She nodded.

'There is a saying in these parts, Temple, that who-

72

ever rides a tiger cannot dismount. To love a person, or a place, is to ride a tiger.'

'It sounds so savage, put like that.' Her hazel eyes dwelt wide and distressed on Alan's face, and at once he took a step towards her and was standing rather close to her as Ryk came back into the room. Something glimmered over his arm, and Temple drew away rather hurriedly from Alan, as if she feared that Ryk would think them too intimate, too soon.

'This will save you from taking a chill, Miss Lane.' Ryk threw the glimmering thing about her shoulders, a shawl of Indian silk, the colour of a red tulip. He brushed his hand along the fringe of the shawl, and then he looked directly at Temple, as if curious, as if it had touched his iron loneliness to enter a room and find a girl and a man on the verge of an embrace – almost.

'You look like a favourite slave in that red silk,' Alan smiled.

The rich silk caressed her bare arms, and a scent clung to it, evasive, faintly musky. 'Thank you, *meneer*. I'll bring it back to you tomorrow—'

'Keep it.' He spoke with a careless indifference. 'Prince Chai was here with a girl not so long ago – she left it behind and I am sure has plenty of other silks and furbelows to keep her happy.'

Temple bit her lip, vexed with herself for thinking the shawl had belonged to one of the two women he had loved. It was merely the silk wrap of a prince's girl-friend. The silk in which a favourite was always wrapped.

'Goodnight, *meneer*.' She gave Ryk her coolest look, and then she thought of him as a boy, very fair and with a pair of grey eyes, and of the things that had hardened him. She folded the shawl about her so that the red silk flamed against the pale skin of her throat. 'I should like to see the peacocks – when you have time to show me.'

He bowed, cool and aloof, and stood in the courtyard as she and Alan walked away towards the *laan*. Alan carried a lantern and it was as if they had stepped back into another century. His free hand found her elbow beneath the fringe of the shawl, and everything was still but for the distant chorus of the *kikkers* in the rice terraces.

'He's lonely,' she said to Alan. 'The loneliest person I've ever known.'

'He loved a girl – did you know?'

'Yes.'

'He can't forget the disaster in which she was killed. He blames himself for Marta's death – he rides a tiger and he can't dismount because it would mean being torn from his dream.'

'Yes.' Her voice was a husky whisper in the dark, which the lantern broke into patches of mysterious light. Fireflies burned briefly among the trees.

'You are one of those who feels the hurts of others, aren't you, Temple?' Alan stopped walking, tall in the dark, a pale cloud of moonflowers drifting across their path and scenting the air. Moonflowers – to bring back an unfaithful love. Temple tautened, and her lantern-lit eyes met Alan's.

'Yes, I'm a sensitive fool,' she said. 'A man at Lumbaya managed to hurt me, and so I feel sorry for others who have been hurt.'

'Only sorry?' Alan quizzed her. 'Ryk van Helden is all man, and the *tuan besar* with a lot of power to impress a girl. You could get hurt again—'

'Don't say that!' Temple drew away sharply and found she had backed against a tree. Alan took advantage quickly, and before she could stop him he had kissed the peak of hair above her eyes.

'Don't be afraid,' he murmured. 'I'm not the sort who goes in for breaking hearts.'

'I don't intend to let that happen again.' She tried to

74

draw away, but he forced her gently to remain where she was.

'Did that young man at Lumbaya break your heart, Temple? Or did he disillusion you?'

She sighed and relaxed against the tree, for being alone with the doctor did not really alarm her. She liked him. Liked his whimsical blue eyes, and the fact that they could talk together without tension creeping in. The night wind ruffled the trees, and as the leaves shifted and stirred she saw the stars glimmering through.

'Every star a shining spirit or soul,' said Alan, following her gaze. 'Everything in the East is imbued with symbolism, and somehow one is more aware of the fundamental things. One lives closer to nature, to the sea and the soil and the menace of a sudden storm – life takes on a dramatic quality.

'And this you would miss in America,' she smiled.

'I'd stifle.'

'What of your family?'

'I have a free-thinking mother, thank heaven. My sisters are married and have made me an uncle several times over.'

'Don't you intend to marry?' she asked, and it did not occur to her that the question might sound flirtatious.

'It's a basic drive,' he said, 'something most of us get around to needing. But finding the right partner is not all that easy. You shake the apple-tree when you're young and gobble up those who fall fast and easy, but as you get older you begin to realize that it's the apples that cling to the bough that are the sweetest.'

His eyes flicked Temple, who clung against the trunk of the tree, scarlet-shawled and pensive. 'There's honey in you, Temple Lane – with a bite to it.'

'I think I would bite if someone tried to take away the security I have found in being free of love,' she retorted.

'My dear girl,' he laughed, 'do you really mean what

75

you say? Life without loving someone can be lonely – you have seen Ryk, who will probably never marry but who will live out his dream to the bitter end.'

Temple shivered and thought of Ryk wandering through the large and lonely rooms of the palace, remembering the things he and Marta had talked about at Leyden, the plans they had made, the happiness they had been so sure of. He would enter the blue and gold room, and each creak of a chair, each movement of a blind, would be to him the presence of a ghost.

'I'm cold,' Temple said. 'Shall we go?'

Soon they reached the teahouse, which stood shadowed and curly-roofed beneath the stars. 'A romantic place to live in,' Alan remarked. 'You are not alone here?'

'No, I'm not alone. I have a house girl named Mei.'

'Mei Flower?' An odd note crept into the doctor's voice. 'Do you like her – what I mean is do you find her easy to get along with?'

'I find her pretty, but not all that easy to talk to,' Temple admitted.

'Yes, she's pretty – like waxen frangipani.' Alan studied the teahouse, with its shaded veranda and pagoda roof, and clusters of pale temple flower. 'When Ryk first brought her to the island – he's fond of collecting waifs and strays, eh? – I thought she might like to help at the hospital. I suggested this to her, but the girl said she didn't like being among the sick. Some people don't, but Mei said it in a way I didn't much like. Of course, in front of Ryk she's the essence of demure gratitude.'

'She keeps the teahouse spotless,' said Temple, 'and the things about her which I find disturbing could be pure imagination on my part—'

'What things?' Alan demanded.

'Oh, things that wouldn't worry a man. A spider nest in the frangipani which she didn't mention, and the feeling that she stalked me to the palace this evening. I think she's got it into her head that I'm a sort of – rival.'

'You mean she's jealous?' Alan stared down at Temple, the cleft of a frown between his brows. 'I've got a good mind to ask Ryk to give you another house girl—'

'No, please.' Temple touched his arm. 'Mei resents me a little at present, but she'll soon come to realize that I mean nothing to Mijnheer van Helden.'

'Mijnheer?' Alan mocked quietly. 'Do you find it hard to call him by his name?'

'Impossible.'

'Would you find it equally impossible to call me Alan?'

'I'll think about it.' She drew away from him and mounted the veranda steps.

'Come to the hospital tomorrow and meet some of my patients,' he coaxed. 'Lontah, the wife of the village headman, is expecting her first child at any time and she'll appreciate a visit from you. Then there's Tofan, a little boy I recently operated upon. Will you pay us a visit, Temple?'

'I'd love to.' Temple opened the screen door that led into the teahouse. 'It will be in the afternoon. I have some work I want to get through in the morning.'

'Ryk was lucky to find you. He said you were running away from an unhappy situation and that you met on the *Egret*. I'm glad. Now when I come to Bayanura I shall have something to look forward to.'

'Alan—'

'I like the way you say my name.'

'You Americans are incorrigible!'

'You English girls are so cool.' He bowed and his teeth glimmered in a smile. 'I'll see you tomorrow. Maybe I'll take you for a flip in my flying machine. The Java Sea islands take on strange shapes seen from the air. Would you come, or would you be nervous?'

'Only if that machine of yours had automatic controls.'

He laughed. 'You English girls are so – challenging.'

'Goodnight, Dr. Kinraid,' she said firmly.

'Goodnight, Temple Lane.'

She entered the teahouse and stood just inside the screen door, listening until Alan's footsteps had died away across the compound. He was an attractive person, she thought, as she let the scarlet shawl fall slowly from her shoulders.

CHAPTER SEVEN

THE bungalow hospital was situated in the *kampong* where the people of the village had their palm and bamboo houses, eaved by a burnt-gold thatch.

The hospital was thatched and shady, with a veranda supported upon teakwood posts, where several of Dr. Kinraid's patients lay in long rattan chairs. They gazed curiously at Temple as she mounted the steps, and even as she smiled and murmured, *'Selamat siang,'* a small boy in one of the chairs let out a howl as the head came off the toy tiger he was playing with. He threw it angrily and it landed at Temple's feet. She bent and picked up the headless toy and took it across to the child. His tears of petulance lay like beads on his thin cheeks, and he stared at Temple with wet brown eyes.

'Siapa namamu?' she asked. She asked him his name in the local dialect, of which she was acquiring a few handy words, but the strangeness of her clothes and the whiteness of her skin made the boy shy and he wouldn't tell her.

'Is it Tofan?' She smiled down at him and picked up the tiger's head. *'Harimau itu* needs a bandage for his poor head.' She touched gently the boy's bandaged head – a wad of cotton wool was taped across his right ear – and indicated that she would bind the head of his toy. She pointed to the doorway of the hospital. 'Tiger needs *obat.'*

'Obat,' the boy echoed. Medicine. Suddenly like a ray of sunshine a smile spread across his face. 'Tofan *nakal,'* he chuckled.

'Yes, Tofan naughty.' She smiled and touched his cheek. 'I'll take *harimau itu* to see the *dokter.'*

Tofan blinked his long eyelashes, and then he giggled and in an access of shyness he buried his face in his pillow. Temple smiled as she entered the single ward of the bamboo hospital, a clean white room furnished with net-draped beds, small lockers, and ceiling fans. A couple of patients were fast asleep in their beds, and Temple made her way quietly to the swing-doors at the end of the ward.

She found herself in a corridor that smelled of ether and carbolic soap. There was a door with the word Theatre on it, and another bearing the word Dispensary.

Temple tapped upon the door of the dispensary.

'*Silakan masuk!*' a voice called out.

Temple opened the door, and a slender, white-coated figure swung round from a table on which stood several bottles, a small weighing-machine, and a bunsen-burner. Around the walls were bamboo shelves filled with more bottles, all of them labelled.

The young man smiled and bowed. '*Selamat datang,*' he said, and introduced himself as Khun Lan, male nurse and dispenser at the hospital. He spoke English almost perfectly, and he informed her that the doctor had gone to see the headman and would be back shortly. 'The *nangsau* would like some tea?'

'That would be welcome,' she smiled. 'But first do you think you could give me some bandage so I can bind up Tofan's tiger for him?'

'Perhaps the *nangsau* would allow me?' Khun Lan took the toy and examined it, then with deft brown hands he taped the head to the striped body and shot a gleaming smile at Temple as he finished off the operation with a strip of bandage.

'Tofan is convalescent and inclined to become fretful,' he said. 'The doctor operated upon him for a mastoid and we have been inclined to spoil him. There, now his tiger looks as if he has been operated upon.'

'Thank you, Khun Lan, you have made a good job of that.'

'Will the *nangsau* take her tea on the veranda?'

'Please.' Temple glanced round the dispensary, which was as neat and orderly as the young Siamese who worked among the pills and powders and dark-hued medicines. 'You come from Thailand, don't you, Khun Lan?'

'I have that honour.' He bowed again. 'The *nangsau* has been to my land?'

'No, but I have heard that it's very charming and picturesque.'

'No doubt you have seen *The King And I*?' Khun Lan smiled with a sudden worldliness. 'A most colourful film, but Siam is much advanced since the days of Anna and her Diary – pretty young girls of the harem are no longer burned for falling in love. I am informed that the *nangsau* is working upon a diary for the Tuan van Helden?'

'Yes. There are about two dozen of them and I am typing them out in manuscript form for Mijnheer van Helden. They were compiled by his ancestress, Polyana, who lived here many years ago.'

'When the Indies were the gold pot of the Dutch.'

'Well, I suppose you could put it like that.' She met Khun Lan's dark eyes and detected in them a flicker of animosity. It had not been there before Ryk had been brought into the conversation! 'They were very colourful days, Khun Lan, and I must admit that I'm enjoying my work on the diaries.'

'To live here in the Indies must make a great change for you, *Nona* Lane?'

'Indeed it's quite exciting.' To be addressed as *Nona* was rather appealing; it was a much more attractive word than Miss. 'I shall be very sorry to leave when my work is finished. The scenery is so exotic, and I love the smell of the tea valley when the evening dews begin to fall. It rises up and comes right in through the windows of the teahouse.'

'Ah yes, the teahouse.' Khun Lan's eyes were suddenly veiled. 'And now I must see about making a pot of tea for the *nangsau*. I will bring it to the veranda, with little rice cakes.'

'*Terima kasih*.' She smiled. 'Do I say "thank you" with the proper accent?'

Khun Lan smiled and bowed her out of the dispensary. As she made her way out of the hospital to the veranda, she pondered the change that had come into Khun Lan's manner at her mention of the teahouse. What was it about the place that made him close his slanting eyelids in such a secretive way?

Tofan lost his shyness when he saw his bandaged tiger. '*Lutju*,' he laughed, and held it up for the others on the veranda to see and to smile at.

'Funny tiger,' Temple agreed, and she was sitting on the foot of Tofan's long chair when Alan Kinraid came bounding up the veranda steps, looking tanned and fit in a white shirt and khaki cotton slacks.

'Hullo there!' He came along the veranda with a delighted smile, and Temple was conscious of dark eyes upon them as he took hold of her hand and gave it a welcoming squeeze. 'Sorry I wasn't here to show you around, but I've been to have a few words with the headman. His wife is nearly forty, you see, and this will be her first child. She's remarkably calm, but he's as on thorns as if about to give birth to the baby himself.'

'Proves he loves her.' Temple smiled and thought how blue the doctor's eyes were.

'*Dokter*,' the boy showed Alan his invalid tiger. '*Wanita membetulkan*.'

'Woman put right, eh?' Alan shot a grin at Temple. '*Namanja Nona* Temple.'

'Tem-pel.' The boy cocked his cheeky head on one side and grinned at her. 'Tem-pel *tjantik.*'

'He says you're beautiful,' Alan said dryly.

'Well, that's the nicest thing a young man ever said to me. *Terima kasih,* Tofan. You're going to be quite a lad with the ladies when you grow up.'

He nodded in agreement, and then he put a hand to his bandaged ear and gave it a rub. '*Telinga gatal, dokter.*'

'The ear itches,' Alan told Temple, who looked concerned. 'Soon I shall be able to send this young man home to his family – ah, here comes Khun Lan with our tea. Have you met my right-hand man, Temple?'

She smiled and nodded as Khun Lan wheeled a tea-trolley on to the veranda. Tea was handed round, along with little rice cakes, and soon Temple had been introduced to most of the patients. They obviously thought the world of their *dokter,* and in the midst of that tea party Temple thought of Ryk van Helden. The sun was turning from gold to flame above the tea valley, and Ryk would be making his way home to the palace, there to drink his sundowner all alone.

'Loneliness becomes a lover, solitude a darling sin.' He had said that last night, and it was as if he had grown invulnerable and needed none of the warmth and the love that was so much a part of the life of the islanders. He stood apart from the warm centre of their lives. He was respected as the *tuan besar,* but he was not expected to relax among them as Alan did.

'*Selamat tinggal.*' She waved goodbye to Alan's patients, and he climbed with her the hilly path that led home to the teahouse. The sun was melting into the swift tropical dusk, and as they reached the rim of the valley they stood gazing down at the village, where the cooking fires began to flicker among the shadows.

'I'm going to have to put off our spin over the islands

until after Lontah's baby is born.' Alan fired a cigarette. 'The islanders are grand people, aren't they? They live by the belief that happiness comes from within ourselves and that only the foolish try to seek it elsewhere.'

'They have the capacity to love and to give, and they are not envious of their neighbours,' Temple said quietly. 'One could become too fond of life on Bayanura.'

'Don't think ahead,' Alan said. 'Live each day as it comes. Savour it as you would a sugared lotus pod, so that not a drop of your happiness is lost. You were happy to meet my patients, eh?'

'Yes, especially Tofan. I'm afraid I have a softness for small, saucy boys.'

'It's nice to be called beautiful,' Alan teased her.

She laughed and put her head back and breathed the scents of the tea valley. A breeze fluttered the long leaves of the palms and the banyans; overhanging shaggy leaves bent in all directions like heavy lengths of grass. Lovely wild island, spiced with the unexpected.

'What would my aunt say? And Dora and Cheryl, my two cousins? To them I was the general skivvy.'

'Cinderella?' he murmured.

'Whose Prince was not as charming as she had imagined.'

'Forget him,' Alan advised. 'If he had been worth loving, you'd be with him right now. The fundamental woman in you, Temple, has not yet been stirred awake. You're waiting for that.'

'Panting,' she scoffed. 'Listen! Whatever's that strange noise?'

It wailed up to them from the valley, like a banshee.

'It's for me.' Alan dropped his cigarette to the ground and put it out under his shoe. 'A member of the headman's family is blowing a conch-shell to let me know I'm wanted. Lontah is either about to give birth, or her husband is having another attack of the wobblies.'

84

'Good luck, Alan.'

'Yes, let's hope it's the baby. Will you be okay on your own?'

'Of course. I'm not a baby!'

'You're pretty innocent.' He touched her shoulder and ran his warm hand down her arm. 'Innocence alarms a man, disarms him, and then charms him.'

'And then we're back to square one,' she said lightly. 'Presumably charmed, and no longer alarmed, the man tries to disarm the girl?'

'At the moment,' as the conch-shell emitted another wail, 'I haven't the time to try and disarm you, Temple. Will you swim with me tomorrow? I should be free to meet you on the beach, for I have an idea Lontah is going to produce this baby *terlambat*.'

'Which means?'

'After the appointed time.'

'The poor husband will be a nervous wreck.'

'Mmmm.' Alan took her fingers into his hand and seemed to enjoy for a moment the deceptive fragility of the female hand. 'Women amaze me. They're so calm in the face of the big issues, but let a mouse show a whisker and they're on a chair screaming the roof off.'

'Isn't that skittish streak good for the male ego?'

'Women!' He carried her hand to his lips and kissed it lightly. 'Meet me on the beach in the morning, eh?'

'All right.'

'Not panting?' His fingers were over her pulse. 'No, quite steady.'

'I told you, Doctor, that I'm the girl in armour.'

'Don't wear it tomorrow, *wanita*. One of those bathing sarongs on a girl is always good for my circulation.'

'I think a bathing suit will be safer,' Temple rejoined, a warmth in her cheeks as she thought of the previous evening, when she had lost her sarong in the water and Ryk van Helden had come along to witness her predicament.

'Beware, Temple,' Alan spoke laughingly. 'The girl in retreat arouses the hunter in a man.'

'That poor man down in the village will blow his wits out in a minute.' She pulled her hand free of his. 'Goodnight, Alan.'

'*Selamat malam.*' He waved his hand and went bounding down the hillside, and with a smile Temple turned to make her way home to the teahouse.

A tropical twilight is as swift-falling as a dark cloak, and Temple was enwrapped by the shadows, and her nerves were attuned to the mysterious whistlings and flutterings that went on in the groves of trees and thickets. The falling night was filled with the chorus of the cicadas, who would sing frantically before falling suddenly silent.

To reach the teahouse she had to pass the fruit orchards bordering the palace, dark and redolent of pineapples, melons, pomelo, bananas, papaya, and the sour, spiked durian.

She wished she had her hand torch with her . . . and then as plainly as last night she heard a movement among the trees. She glanced round sharply, and the trees took mysterious shapes around her. It could have been her imagination playing tricks with her, but why did she feel so cold, so aware of something hostile? 'Who's there?' she cried out.

Silence, but for the cicadas. Silence that was more stealthy than the tread she had heard. Silence that *breathed*.

She began to run, blundering her way past the trees that reached out, brushing at the clustering leaves, and the lianas that looped traps for her feet. Suddenly something gripped her ankle and she was falling before she could save herself.

86

She saw stars ... she literally saw stars as her head came in contact with the trunk of a tree. She heard a cry and knew it to be her own as she passed out cold. . . .

Something stung her nostrils and she gasped for breath as the ammonia brought her round, and she found herself stretched out on a divan. She blinked, and even that was enough to make her head pound. 'Oh – my head!'

'You have quite a bump, *meisje*.' A strong arm slipped about her shoulders and she groaned as she was made to sit up and drink something that burned her throat. 'Ammonia?' she choked.

'No, silly child, whisky.'

Her senses were clearing and the man's face came into clearer focus as she looked at him. Tawny mane of hair, dark triangular patch over one eye, a hard chin with a crooked cleft in it. 'Oh – you!'

'I did not swing a club and knock you unconscious,' he was looking sardonic as he examined the bruise upon her forehead. 'This needs bathing – lie back against the cushions while I fetch some permanganate in water to cleanse the edges of that bruise.'

She did as she was told and watched him stride from the room. Somehow it did not surprise her that Ryk had found her knocked out in his woods. He seemed fated to be her reluctant knight errant.

'*Ouch!*' It hurt even to smile a little, and she had her eyes closed as Ryk came back into the room. He bathed her forehead with care and few words, but Temple felt that keen grey eye upon her and she knew that he was merely giving her time to regain her scattered wits.

'Does that feel easier?' he asked. He set aside the bowl, and stood confronting her with his hands thrust into the pockets of his jungle-cloth trousers. His white shirt was deeply open at his tanned throat, and in her weak state Temple had to admit to herself that he was a dangerously exciting man to look at. An enigma who

87

no longer offered his broad shoulder to a woman to lean against.

'Yes, it's taken the sting out, thank you.'

'Good. And now I should like an explanation as to how you came to be alone and unconscious in the woods.'

'I – I was on my way home to the teahouse. I had tea at the hospital with Dr. Kinraid, you see, and he was seeing me home when he was called back to the village—' She moistened her lips and looked away from Ryk's disconcerting gaze. 'A liana tripped me, I think, and I hit my head against a tree.'

'You were in a hurry to get home?'

'Yes. It was dark a-and I thought I heard something— Her eyes flashed to his face, and she winced as the quick movement shot a pain through her head. 'Was it you I heard, *meneer*?'

'Was it I who gave you a scare?' He frowned. 'The cub was out in the woods and I went to call him in. I found him licking your face, and it could be said that it was you who gave me a scare.'

'Aren't you sure, *meneer*?'

He didn't smile at her quip, but looked rather forbidding with the lamplight on the hard lines of his face, his chin dented by shadow.

'One hears strange rustlings at night,' he said crisply. 'There is no one on this island who would want to hurt you, and you must not allow your imagination to run away with you.'

'I'll try not to,' she said meekly, and all the time she was thinking of Mei. Mei with her small face like a pale golden mask, and her eyes that followed one from behind long silky lashes. Mei, who wanted this brooding tiger of a man.

'I – I should be getting back to the teahouse,' she said, and was about to stir from among the cushions of the divan when Ryk bent over her and pushed her back

88

again, quite gently. Her eyes met his, deeply hazel beneath the bruise on her forehead. Her dark hair was rumpled, and in her shirt and pants she was slender as a boy, and helpless as a girl from that touch of his.

'I will have supper brought in here,' he said, 'and when you have eaten something and the dizziness has quite passed, I will take you home.'

She couldn't reply to him, she was too conscious of that sunburned hand so close to her. She had never been so aware of a male hand before, strong, work-hardened, and yet capable of being caressive.

'Don't you wish to stay?' He rapped out the words.

'Have I a choice?' She flickered a look at him.

'Of course.' He looked right at her, a quirk to his lips.

'Then I'll stay.'

'The English are not to be forced into anything, eh?' His smile deepened the lines of irony beside his mouth. 'I wonder if you are aware of the demon in the Dutch that wakes slowly?'

'What happens when it awakes?' She could feel her heart beating fast.

'We have our way, regardless of a woman's nay or yea.'

'I think, *meneer*, that you were fashioned for the century in which Laurens van Helden lived.'

'Perhaps.' He inclined his tawny head. 'And you, *meisje*, were you fashioned for the days when you might have been a glove bride?'

'I did in part what Polyana did all those years ago.' She looked at Ryk and could no longer remember Nick all that clearly. 'I travelled out to the Indies to be a bride.'

'And instead you became the *secretaresse* of a Dutchman with an uncertain temper, eh?' He laughed mockingly as he straightened up. 'I will go and tell Ranji that you are staying to supper.'

89

'*Meneer*—'

'Yes?'

'Doesn't Alan – I mean Dr. Kinraid – stay here at the palace?'

'No. There is a small bamboo house attached to the hospital and he prefers to sleep there in case he is needed. A blast on that conch-shell in the middle of the night would wake up the entire valley.'

'What if someone is ill when he's away?'

'There is Khun Lan – and myself.' Ryk gave her a sardonic bow, and then the room was strangely empty, and Temple lay listening to a strange drumming sound. It came from outside the windows of the room, and Temple realized suddenly that it was a tropical downpour she was listening to.

Pounding the flagstones of the palace courtyards, splashing upon the tiered roofs, drowning the *kikkers* in the rice terraces.

Tropical rains that could drown a man . . . rains that sometimes went on for hours . . . and here she was alone at the palace with Ryk van Helden.

CHAPTER EIGHT

THE heavy rain continued all through their meal. Ryk had a table set in front of the divan and there they ate their supper of soup, fried chicken with sliced, golden-brown sweet potatoes, and a gingery sauce if required.

Temple's head still ached, and the continuing sound of the rain played a little on her nerves, but the food was good and she was quite hungry.

Ranji brought fruit and coffee, and he informed Ryk that one of the courtyards was filling with water owing to a blocked drain. 'They should be kept clear, man!' Ryk strode out of the room, followed by an apologetic Ranji.

Temple listened to the men splashing about outside, and it frightened her a little that so much water could pour from the skies so suddenly. It made her aware of the violence underlying the beauty of the island. Reminded her of the volcano that towered over the valley and the jungly hills, and the beach of white-hot sand. It was no wonder that emotions were always on tiptoe, and that a word, a look, a movement in the woods could cause a sudden flight into panic – like a bird that flies out suddenly, with a blind flutter of wings.

She took in the room, with its patina of things from another age, and then Ryk returned and the inanimate things seemed to come alive again.

His hair was dark from the rain, and she poured him a cup of coffee and watched him drink it. 'I have to be behind everyone,' he grumbled. 'These people let things slide unless you watch them.'

'The rain is heavy.' She cast a nervous glance at the windows. 'Is it likely to hold up – tonight?'

'Most unlikely.' He was cutting the rough outer skin

91

from a mangosteen and she caught the glint in his eye as he cut the fig-like fruit and handed her a piece. 'The palace is full of empty rooms, so I am sure we'll be able to fix you up for the night.'

'But—'

'It will not be the first time you have slept in pyjamas of mine.' He bit into his piece of fruit and she saw the white glimmer of his teeth. 'Or are you afraid of offending convention by spending the night in the house of a bachelor?'

'If the rain continues at this pace, then I shall have no choice.'

'I remember that you had little choice on the steamer – ah, but I am forgetting that everyone thought you a boy.'

'I wish—'

'What do you wish, *meisje*?' He sat down in a wide-shouldered chair and took a cheroot from the box on a table beside him. As he fired the tip, he watched her across the flame of his lighter. 'That the people we know could live up to our ideals?'

'It would surely be impossible, even a little cruel, to expect our friends to be faultless,' she argued.

'Did you not expect that of the young man at Lumbaya?'

'No, I didn't.' Her eyes lit up with anger. 'I expected Nick to abide by the promises he made, that's all. I could have forgiven him the other girl—'

'Are you sure?' Ryk drawled. 'Some women find it the hardest thing of all to forgive, that a man can love two women at the same time.'

'Love?' she echoed. 'I would hardly call it that!'

'Need – loneliness – they can wear the shape of love.'

'What of a woman's need for romantic love?' she shot back at him. 'We like to touch the stars, even though we have to come down to earth.'

'How young you are!' Suddenly his face was rather harsh as he arose from his chair and went over to the cabinet on which stood decanters and glasses. He cradled a pair of flute glasses in his hand as he poured a dark wine into them. He brought them over to the divan, and Temple's hand felt a little unsteady as she took one of the glasses from his hand.

The teakwood door was closed, and the drumming of the rain seemed to emphasize their silence as they drank their wine. The lamplight was almost too intimate, and there were shadows in the corners of the room.

'By the way, I found something of Polyana's that might interest you.' He opened the cabinet with the peacocks and the flowers painted upon its panels, and took from it an oblong box. He brought it to Temple and she saw that it had painted scenes upon it, faded but still discernible as wedding scenes.

'This is an old Dutch marriage casket,' he wound the key in the lid and as he opened the box a tune tinkled out. 'A musical and jewel box.'

She held it and peered inside eagerly. 'Polyana mentions this box in her diaries,' she said in awe. 'She kept it beside her bed, and it even travelled with her when she took sea voyages with Laurens in one of his sailing ships. *Meneer*, there is something wrapped in a piece of silk!'

'*Ja.*' He took out the small package and unwrapped it. Something gleamed orange and emerald in his fingers, and Temple saw that it was a necklace of oval gems mounted on a silver chain. Old-fashioned, utterly charming, a trinket that had once adorned the neck of Polyana van Helden.

Ryk's fingers played with the necklace while the tune of the musical box tinkled between them. 'Moonstones,' he said. 'Gems made to enchant – like some women.'

Temple didn't dare to lift her gaze from the necklace

to his face, for she was quite certain that she would see there an expression of irony, pain, anger even that he should be showing these things to her instead of the girl he would have married.

'Would you like to try the necklace on?' he asked abruptly.

Temple looked at him then, daring the mockery she might see in his expression. If it was there, he moved too quickly for her to glimpse it. He was at the side of the divan, bending over her, fastening the moonstones about her neck. They gleamed against her white skin, still warm from his touch.

'Come.' He took her by the hand and made her rise from the divan, and a bewildered moment later she found herself standing in front of a wall mirror, with Ryk reflected tall and quizzical behind her.

She felt him close to her, lean and hard-muscled from work in the open all day. She heard him breathing, and had never been more aware of the tigerish grace and power of the man, and of his enigmatic personality.

'Would you like to keep the moonstones?' he asked casually.

She stared at his reflection in the mirror, shy of him, bewildered by him

'I am sure Polyana would like to know that they adorn once more the neck of a young English girl.' He smiled briefly, and then looked stern again.

'I – I couldn't possibly accept them!' Temple began to fumble with the catch, and at once he gripped her hands and swung her round to face him. She struggled to get away, and then saw something in his face that half frightened her. As she felt the threatening crush of his fingers, she knew that a man who lived on an island could not be called fully tamed!

'Do you regard a gift as first cousin to seduction?' he drawled.

'The moonstones belong in your family,' she said desperately. 'You're giving them away because you think you will never want to marry again—'

It was too late to retract. She saw that as his face darkened, as he jerked her against him, painfully. 'Don't!' she gasped.

'Don't, *meisje*?' he mocked. 'Who is to stop me? This is my home and we are alone in it but for my servants. A deluge pours down outside, and no one would hear your cries if I kissed you.'

She was beyond even a whisper as he held her within the circle of one arm, and tipped her head back into the cradle of his other arm. She lost her breath at the mere thought of feeling his sardonic lips against her own.

He stared down at her, tawny hair tousled above the lean face, and the dark triangular patch behind which the grey eye was sealed. Then suddenly with a laugh he put her from him. 'Take that look out of your eyes,' he ordered. 'I am well aware that the eye-patch makes me sinister to *jong vrouwen*.'

He turned from her and took another cheroot. His lighter clicked impatiently as he fired the tip. 'I wanted you to have the moonstones because you are doing good work on the diaries.' Smoke jetted from his nostrils. 'I cannot wear them, *meisje*, and I really think you should accept them after I took the trouble to clean and polish them.'

She caught the whimsical note in his voice, but the blind side of his face was towards her and she could not read his expression. 'If I sound ungrateful, *meneer*, perhaps it's because I'm not used to – to receiving presents. Especially a present of moonstones.'

'Poor foundling!' He drew on his cheroot and smoke wreathed about his tawny head. 'You are starved of kindness, aren't you? Like a little cat who backs away from the saucer of cream in case a kick should follow it.'

She sat down because she felt rather shaky. The rain splashed down the windows, and a pagoda clock chimed softly. She counted the strokes absently, and leaned back in the wings of Ryk's great Dutch chair. The moonstones lay cool, now, against the skin of her throat. Tears burned behind her lowered eyelids.

'Your head is drooping, *jonkvrouw*.' He had turned to look at her. '*Je moet naar bed*.'

She glanced up and her eyes were over-large in her face, pale but for the bruise upon her forehead. 'Thank you for the moonstones, *meneer*. They'll always remind me of Bayanura.'

'You speak as if you were leaving tomorrow,' he said dryly. 'Have I alarmed you to such a degree?'

It was impossible to put a name to the feelings he aroused – was it fascination, or was it fear – or a mingling of the two?

'You think me arrogant?' He quirked a flaxen eyebrow and stood tall and strong in front of her, a man who had cut himself off from the gentler feelings and had let himself become armoured.

'Don't the Chinese say there is a tiger in every man?' she murmured.

'A tiger, an ass, and a nightingale.' His smile was sardonic. 'A bed has been prepared for you, and you really look as if you need a good night's sleep—'

She glanced towards the windows and listened to the hammering rain. The night was drowning in rain, the trees were threshing in a cold wind, and suddenly she shivered.

'The rain will not stop until morning, *meisje*, and I don't propose to go out in it again.' He stubbed out his cheroot. 'Please to come with me.'

Temple got to her feet . . . and suddenly the room went round and she would have fallen but for the strong arms that caught hold of her and lifted her.

She was dizzy, helpless in Ryk's arms, close to his hard brown throat, inches from the lips that looked as though they would be without mercy....

'I – I'm all right—'. She was uncertain whether it was her head or her heart that pounded so.

He didn't listen to her, and she felt herself carried across the hall as easily as if she weighed no more than a little cat. Up the curving staircase they went, until the hall below was a sea of marble and shadow and the glimmer of bronze from the big gong, and the figure of the goddess of mercy.

Long ago in that hall a Javanese prince would have watched his dancing girls. One of them would have attracted him, and when the dancing was over she would have been taken to his presence.

Temple's drowsy hazel eyes dwelt on the cleft chin above her head. Fierce, haunted, unpredictable man!

'If you are still feeling the effects of that bump tomorrow, then Alan Kinraid must have a look at you.' Ryk was now carrying her along a cool, marble floored corridor. It was lit by lamps that gleamed like dark jewels and cast coloured shadows that outlined the thrust of Ryk's cheekbones, and emphasized the sinister eye-patch.

'You must think me very foolish to run into a tree.'

'I often think you foolish, *meisje*.' He smiled down mockingly into her drowsy eyes. 'Did you really think that I would kiss you? That the privilege of my position gives me the right to think that any girl is for my taking?'

'Getting bumped on the head must have scattered my wits. As if you would want to kiss me!' And then her breath seemed lost in her throat as he cradled her in one arm and thrust open a bedroom door with his free hand. He carried her into the room and laid her down on a great carved bed, with a netting canopy affixed to a ring in the ceiling.

For a brief moment Ryk's hands lingered upon her

97

shoulders, and she felt beneath her the sinking depths of the bed. The lamp was lit, casting a warm glow over Temple, revealing her ruffled hair, her questioning eyes . . . her hands that clenched the silk of the coverlet.

'You have pyjamas and a toothbrush.' Ryk swung away towards the door. 'The bathroom is directly across the corridor.'

'Thank you.' She sat up, a slim, lost figure in the centre of the great bed. Its tall carved posts reared towards the ceiling.

'You look lost in that Dutch bed.' Ryk stood in the doorway, his hands thrust into the pockets of his jungle-cloth slacks, his skin looking dark against the whiteness of his shirt. 'Sleep well in it, child.'

'*Saya tuan besar.*' She smiled and bowed her head like a little slave, and looked ready to fall asleep at any moment.

'*Goede nacht, meisje.*' He bowed back at her, then withdrew and closed the door behind him.

As always when he left a room, he left it feeling empty. Temple slipped off the bed and found dark silk pyjamas folded upon a cane chair, and a toothbrush and toilet things upon the bedside table. The rain still fell, and after she returned from the bathroom she lay listening to the downpour.

Mei would guess that she was spending the night at the palace, and Temple suddenly pulled the silk coverlet to her chin and felt again that cold sensation of having made an enemy.

All was still when Temple awoke. The rain had died away in the night, but the birds had not found the spirit to come out and sing. The sunshine fell in thin, fretted patterns upon the floor, and her head no longer felt light and heavy at the same time.

There was a tap on her door, and it opened to admit

Ranji. He carried a teatray to her bedside. '*Selamat pagi, mem.*' He showed his gold teeth in a smile, and poured her tea into a small bowl lacquered with blue flowers. He handed her the tea-bowl with a bow, and watched as she took a long, satisfying drink.

'*Mem* take *makan-pagi* here?' he asked.

'No, out in the sunshine.'

'With *tuan*?' Ranji gazed straight at her with dark, innocent eyes.

'Yes.' She tucked her nose in her tea-bowl, and didn't look up again until the white-coated, black-capped figure had slipped quietly away. Then she took a look round the bedroom, with its mingling of Dutch baroque and golden cane. Its screens with birds in silk-thread motion, its rugs that had turned ivory-coloured with age. On the cane bedside table there was a lamp like a brass slipper – one could rub it and make a wish!

What would I wish? she wondered as she poured herself a second bowl of tea; fragrant, grown in the valley below the palace. She sipped it, and tried to bring to mind the face of Nick Hallam. But it was blurred, overshadowed by the faces of the people she had met here on Bayanura. It no longer hurt her to think about him. He had gone out of her life, and now it amazed her that for five years she had thought herself in love with him.

She slipped out of bed and stood barefooted in the long silk pyjama jacket with the dragons on the pockets. She could see herself in the mirror of the dressing-table, an urchin figure, the sleeves of the jacket hanging down over her hands, and a decided bump on her forehead.

She found her sandals, and made a dart for the bathroom. The door swung open, a tall figure emerged in the wake of bath steam. Ryk, showered and shaved, with a rough robe swinging back from a golden torso and dark silk Chinese trousers.

'*Goede morgen.*' He was quite unruffled by the

encounter, but Temple had to force herself to look composed.

'Good morning, *meneer*.'

He flicked a glance over her slim, bare-legged figure in his pyjama jacket. 'We make an economical pair,' he quipped. 'I never sleep in a top, and you evidently don't sleep in bottoms.'

'No,' she said, and her fingers caught at the hem of his jacket.

'How's the head this morning?' He quizzed the bump on her forehead. 'Bathe that with some cool water, it will help to take it down.'

The next moment he strode off, leaving her to escape into the bathroom and to lean her back against the door while she caught her breath. She could smell sandalwood soap, and a tangy shaving lotion. There were large wet footprints on the tiled floor, and the bath was a sunken one of mottled marble, large enough for a couple to swim in.

Temple prepared herself a bath, and found bath-oil in a green container that filled the air with the tang of pine-trees. She stepped down into the tub and lay whipping the water into a lather with her feet.

It was lovely not to be hampered by a narrow white tub, and by her cousins hammering on the door. She splashed as much as she liked, and used Ryk's sandalwood soap with a lavish hand.

She would take Alan's advice and enjoy each day fully and not think of the time when she must leave the island. One thing was certain, she would never return to Alford. Having spread her wings, she would not let her aunt and her cousins clip them for her ever again.

She floated about in Ryk van Helden's big marble tub, one of the perquisites he enjoyed as right-hand man of a Javanese prince, and it felt good to be free of being the orphan cousin who did the chores in return for a bit of charity. She was like a kitten, Ryk van Helden had said, who shied from a saucer of cream in case a kick should follow it.

Strange that he should know how she felt, and yet not really strange at all. War and a rebellion had left him parentless. A plane crash had taken from him the girl he had loved. He understood her plight, and had given her the moonstones because he felt sorry for her.

She towelled herself down, and wrapped in the great coloured towel she returned to her bedroom. There a surprise awaited her in the form of a *kebaya*, a lovely embroidered jacket with pearl buttons, and a long skirt of amber yellow, such as the island women wore. There was also a pair of lacquered sandals.

Temple had often longed to dress up in such clothes, and she hesitated no more than a minute before wrapping herself in the long silk skirt and tucking it in at the front as she had seen it done by Mei. She slipped into the *kebaya*, silky and cool, and her fingers shook a little as she buttoned it up. Then she stepped into the sandals, and studied herself in the mirror.

With her dark hair, and her slender wrists and ankles, she did not look out of place in the garments. They gave her a lissom look, and seemed to bring out the sorcery that lurks sometimes in hazel eyes. Her heart beat excitedly as she picked up the moonstones and fastened them about her throat. They gleamed and blended with the silk, and Temple wondered as she studied her reflection if she would have the nerve to go down to breakfast dressed like this.

There was a tap on the door and she turned nervously to face it as it opened. Ranji appeared, and she saw from his smile that he admired her in the Javanese outfit. '*Tuan* say breakfast ready and that *mem* should come. *Mem* like Java dress?'

She cast a look at the shirt and trews which her

fall in the woods had soiled. 'Yes, Ranji, I like the dress.'

'Then please to follow me.' Ranji bowed her out of the door and escorted her down the winding marble stairs and out of an archway into the sunshine of a terrace that overlooked the valley. Ryk was leaning against the parapet, and he turned as he heard the patter of Temple's sandals. The sun caught his ruddy mane of hair, and he wore a suit of tropical white, tailored perfectly across his broad shoulders.

'So you put it on.' His smile was enigmatical. 'I wondered whether you would dare.'

She walked across the terrace to join him at the parapet, self-conscious, and yet aware that the long silk skirt made her walk with grace. 'You like to challenge me, don't you, *meneer*?' She peered down at the green, misty slopes of the valley. The air was rain-cooled and the sun was bringing out the scents of the flame blossoms, the datura and the tamarinds. She saw a wild hibiscus wedded to the many branches of a banyan tree. A native deer, long-legged, timid and swift, darted out of sight among the trees. An iridescent bee-eater whirred through the air, and scarlet petals lay where the rain had washed them from the flame trees.

Temple savoured the morning air, and saw the rice windmills through the mist that clung to the rice terraces.

'It's beautiful,' she murmured. 'An enchanted valley.'

'Always on Sunday mornings I take my *makan-pagi* on this terrace,' Ryk stood tall beside her. 'From here one can see everything, not only the valley but the cone of the volcano. It just about pierces the mist, do you see? Blue like a sapphire.'

'It's awesome.' Her hand clenched the parapet, pale beside his brown hand. 'The mist over the rice terraces makes them look silvery.'

'It is always misty after a night of rain. Usually it

clears by noon, when the sun is at its zenith.'

'I hope the mist clears. I've promised to go swimming with Alan – Dr. Kinraid.' A warmth came into her cheeks as Ryk turned deliberately to look at her. 'The villagers are very fond of the doctor, aren't they?'

'Alan is not a difficult man to like, or to understand. Come.' Ryk's fingers felt hard as they took hold of her elbow. 'Our breakfast is being brought to the table.'

CHAPTER NINE

A TABLE for two was set on the terrace, and Temple tucked in with appetite as wild doves trilled from their perches on the carved eaves of the palace. Juicy slices of papaya rounded off the meal, and Temple lay back replete in her chair.

'Your appetite is improving.' Ryk stirred sugar into his third cup of black coffee. 'A week ago you were eating like a bird.'

'It's the magic air of Bayanura.' She reached out a lazy hand and plucked an orange peacock flower. 'Will you show me the peacocks, *meneer*?'

'You have a date to go swimming with the good doctor.' A glint of mockery came into Ryk's grey eye. 'Will you wear a sarong?'

'Don't remind me of that incident!' She plucked the petals from the orange flower and could not meet his quizzical glance. 'You promised to show me the peacocks, and I shan't be meeting Alan for another hour or so.'

'He brought me some periodicals from the mainland and I was looking forward to a lazy read in the sun.'

'In that case, I'll leave you in peace.' She rose swiftly to her feet, and in that moment a coloured, whirring flash startled her, so that she took a step backward, unaware that the terrace steps were close behind her. She would have fallen down them if Ryk had not moved with tigerish swiftness and caught hold of her.

'What an impulsive young creature you are!' His fingers gripped and bruised. 'That was a humming-bird, not a stinging-fly.'

'The sting came from you,' she retorted, shaken. 'Please let me go! Y-you're hurting—'

'*Het spijt me.*' He unlocked his grip and stood frowning down at her as she rubbed her arm. 'You are like a child who is always running into danger. A second fall, down stone steps, might have had serious consequences.'

'I don't suppose that would have worried you,' she said, ruffled and robbed of the dignity she had felt earlier in the island dress.

'It would at least be a nuisance to be deprived of a secretary just as work on the diaries is going so well,' he replied cuttingly. 'Why are you so eager to see the pea-cocks?'

'B-because I want them to be part of what I shall remember when the time comes for me to leave the island.' She looked away from him, not wanting him to see how her lips quivered. 'It doesn't matter now. I realize that you want to have a read, and that I'm in the way—'

'No.' He stood barring her way down the steps to the garden. 'If you want so much to see the peacocks, then I shall take you to see them. But let me say this, *meisje*, the beautiful things of this island will be here a hundred years from now – unless the volcano turns angry and destroys us all. Is it that you are merely young that you rush into everything? Or has life taught you too well that rainbows don't last?'

'They don't, *meneer*.' She gazed directly up at him, and saw the harsh lines of suffering stamped about his firm mouth. 'I – I don't want to drag you away from your papers—'

'Ah, but you do, to see the rainbow that the peacock makes when he spreads his tail-feathers. We go this way, and you must be very quiet or the birds will become shy and you will not see their courtship dance.'

Gold and flame petals lay on the path they followed. Leaves and palm fronds had been broken from the trees by the force of the rain in the night, and the songbirds chirped in hiding, while the cicadas seethed with activity in the tall trees.

The depths of the garden held the sounds and the dimness of a jungle, but Temple was not nervous in the way she had been last night. She held her silken skirt above her ankles and walked carefully behind Ryk, who turned every now and again to give her that brief, stern smile of his. Feathery bamboos began to close in around them, and suddenly she gave a start as a harsh cry echoed through the garden. It was the cry of a peacock, and she realized that they were close to where the graceful birds courted the peahens.

Ryk turned and held a finger to his lips. Then he proceeded with caution, holding aside leaves like great shaggy elephant-ears and beckoning Temple to join him in the screen and shadow of a grove of trees heavy with blossom. Datura blossoms, showering pollen upon his shoulders. Temple brushed it off, and then moved delicately away from him as he turned to glance down at her.

The hanging leaves shadowed his face, and the triangular patch was dark against his tanned skin. Temple's heard beat fast, for never before had she been alone with Ryk in so mysterious a place, pagan with the courtship of peacocks, dim and alive with winged creatures and the scents of rain-washed forest flowers.

'Come closer,' he murmured.

She hesitated, and then allowed herself to be drawn near to him. He lifted aside carefully the branch that screened them, and Temple watched fascinated a proud peacock amidst a harem of peahens. His plumage glinted like gems, and then he gave one of those harsh cries and his tail suddenly unfolded and there was a shimmer as of a rainbow in the centre of the grove.

He strutted back and forth, displaying proudly to a small shy peahen his gold-brushed feathers, and the great eye that stood out clearly on the shimmering fan.

He dipped his head. He turned around and flirted the fan. He was so magnificent, and the little peahen so plain and bashful, that Temple couldn't suppress a little laugh.

A hand pressed her waist, warningly. Her lash-veiled glance strayed upwards to the wide shoulders, the cleft chin, the tawny mane of hair. So tall, and with an immobility that suggested power and energy far more potently than if he had been a restless man.

What, she wondered, would it be like to be loved to madness by such a man?

As the thought stirred through her mind, she drew away from contact with him. It was this place that had put such a thought into her mind! The heady datura, the courting peacocks, even the silk that sheathed her body to the ankles and made her feel slightly helpless.

She had wanted to come here, and now she wanted to run away.

'The time's getting on,' she said in a low voice. 'I – I don't want to keep Alan waiting.'

Ryk looked at her, and a sudden cold fire seemed to gleam in his eye. 'I have no wish to keep you from your meeting with him,' he said coldly. 'But let me remind you—'

'I know.' Her smile was nervous, for when Ryk drew himself up like that he was truly formidable. 'The peacocks are fascinating, but it's quite a long walk back to the palace, and then I have to return to the teahouse to collect my bathing things.'

He gazed at her a moment longer, his mouth rather grim, and then he swung on his heel and strode on ahead of her. She followed as quickly as her long silk skirt would allow, and at last they emerged out of the green and seething dimness into the sunlight. Temple leaned against a tree in the courtyard to catch her breath, while Ryk stood frowning at the puddles that lay among the uneven flagstones.

He didn't speak, and his sternness imposed silence upon Temple. How could she tell him that in the woods she had felt aware of him to such a degree that it had frightened her? That never in her life had anyone disturbed her quite so much as he did.

The only way to defend herself from the shocking, terrible urge to kiss the lines in his face, and the scarred eye, had been to run away from being alone with him!

Suddenly he looked at her, and it jarred her heart to see the cruel little quirk to his lips. 'Were you afraid I would lose my head over being alone with you? I thought I had put your fears to rest last night.'

'I have never thought it likely that any man would lose his head over me,' she rejoined. 'Nick Hallam only wanted me because he saw in me a good housekeeper, and maybe a prop, and I'll never let myself be hurt again by the delusion that I could be desired for myself.'

They stared at each other across the sunlit courtyard, a girl sheathed in silk against the plaited trunk of a palm tree, the man with something leashed and tigerish about him. Suddenly there was a flutter and something was caught in the flamy sunlight as it settled on Ryk's shoulder. A gold-winged butterfly ... a messenger from heaven.

Ryk stood very still, and Temple watched as if under a spell as the butterfly hovered on his white-clad shoulder, then at last it fluttered away and was lost among the flowers.

Temple lifted her gaze to Ryk's face, and her heart quickened as she saw the pallor beneath his tan. So he knew the superstition as well, about butterflies being the souls of the beautiful ... and the dead?

'Strange,' he said, and he seemed to gaze at Temple with two blind eyes. 'Today would have been her birthday.'

Temple couldn't speak, she could only watch as he strode out of sight beneath an archway of the palace. The cicadas beat their wings and the hot air was filled with their chirring, but Temple was conscious of nothing save the fact that Ryk had looked at her just now as if she didn't exist.

Temple stirred and felt the silk of her dress catch against the palm tree. She wished to change out of the *kebaya* and long skirt, but her own clothes were in the palace, and somehow she couldn't enter the place again today. She wanted to get away before she encountered Ryk. She wanted to be with Alan Kinraid, who regarded her as a person not as someone to mock; or someone to dictate to.

She was assailed by almost a feeling of homecoming as she reached the compound of the teahouse. She crossed quickly to the veranda, and as she started up the steps, she saw someone watching her through the screen door. She knew it was Mei, and there was nothing she could do but enter the lounge in the garments which had seemed such fun to wear – an aeon ago.

Mei looked at her with inscrutable eyes, but Temple felt the hostility of the other girl, and the veiled contempt. In such clothes as these, Mei had the grace of a flower. Temple had hurried all the way to the teahouse and she was hot, and the skirt hung untidily.

'I am meeting Dr. Kinraid for a swim.' Her hand was on the *chik* and she was about to go along to her bedroom when Mei spoke.

'*Dokter* send message by boy.'

Temple swung to face Mei, who held out a sealed envelope. Temple took it and quickly opened it. Her heart sank as she read the message inside.

'*Sorry, Temple, to break our date. A teak boss on one of the islands has had a serious accident and his foreman has radioed for my help. I am flying over to operate,*

109

see you soon! Regards, Alan.'

So that was that! Alan would not be meeting her for that longed-for swim, and she mustn't be selfish and wish he were here instead of on his way to help someone in vital need.

'Will you be here for *makan-siang, mem*?'

Temple glanced up absently from Alan's note. 'Lunch? Oh – yes. Yes, please, Mei. Dr. Kinraid had to fly to an accident case.'

'I heard the plane leave.' There was in Mei's look a sudden burning darkness, an animosity that would not be concealed. She knew that Temple had been in Ryk's company, and because she was infatuated with him she could think of only one thing that would drown all awareness for a woman. She thought that Temple had been in his arms!

Temple had been in the heart of the palace garden with Ryk, where the seething jungle sounds and the cry of the peacocks had blotted out the sound of Alan's plane as it had flown off over the sea.

'A simple lunch will do, Mei.' Temple tried to speak in a normal tone of voice and to ignore the tension that vibrated between her and the Asian girl. 'I shall go for a swim when the sun has cooled down.'

Mei placed her slender hands together and bowed over them, as inscrutable as a pale golden idol once again. She turned and only the *chik* curtain at the other end of the lounge made any sound as she went through it. The bamboo strips gradually quietened, and there was only the sound of the ceiling fans as Temple stood staring at the sprays of frangipani in a vase on a bamboo table.

Yes, she would go to the beach alone and she would hunt for the ring she had lost the other evening. Her mother's garnet and pearl ring that might have slipped off her finger in the cave where she had changed into the bathing sarong.

Her hands slid down the sides of the long silken skirt ... suddenly this island seemed an unlucky place rather than a magical one.

Or was she feeling despondent because Alan had left? The *chik* danced behind her as she made for her bedroom and a change of dress.

Sea-birds cried through the tendrils of mist that clung to the peaks of the coral reef. The surf broke high over the rocks closer to the beach and made a silken tumult. Crabs scuttled among the palm leaves that the rain had lashed down in the night.

Temple sat on the sands and cradled her knees with her bare arms and the tingle of the sea lingered on her skin as she watched a peak-prowed boat break through the mist far out, and then become lost again as it sailed around the headland. The strange, almost human crying of the sea-birds intensified her feeling of solitude.

Right now Alan would be with his patient. Ryk van Helden would be in his study at the palace, lost in cheroot smoke and memories of the girl whose birthday it would have been. Temple felt again the chill of being looked at so – so blindly, as if no one in the world existed for him but the girl he would never see again; never touch or hold in his arms ever again.

There swept over Temple the loneliness that comes of being left out of the things that matter to other people. If she were a nurse, for instance, she would have flown off with Alan Kinraid on his errand of mercy. . . .

She jumped to her feet and hastened from her thoughts to the cave that yawned in the cliffs above the sloping beach. It was dim and cool inside the cave after the glare of the hot sands, and a pale green sea-light flitted like a goblin about the sea-lichened walls and across the sandy floor. She dressed quickly in her shirt and trews and began to search for her mother's ring.

She longed so much to find it that time was forgotten. Shells came to light as she hunted in the sand and sea-wrack that the tides washed into the cave, pretty things that she polished on the side of her trews and admired with the gravity of a child again.

The sea boomed around the headland, and Temple was so intent on her search that she failed to notice that the sea-birds were crying now about the cliffs, and that puffs of mist were drifting across the mouth of the cave.

Her ring had to be here somewhere, otherwise it was lost to her for ever, and along with it that tangible link with the parents she could not remember.

At last she sat back on her heels and rubbed the small of her back. She became aware that the sea-light had a strange tenuous quality, and she glanced towards the opening of the cave. It should have framed the sea and the sky, and the surf riding white-rimmed over the rocks. Instead there was a white blankness . . . as if the sky had come down and blotted out the beach!

Temple scrambled to her feet and ran to the opening. It was no illusion! The mist had gathered suddenly into a thick, white blanket and the beach was lost under it. It was impenetrable, shutting her in the cave, barring her way. A weird, damp cloud, in which she would be lost if she dared to go out in it. In which she could walk into the rocks, or into the sea.

To be lost in the sea in such a mist would be a nightmare. Fear and exhaustion would soon overpower the hardiest swimmer!

Temple withdrew instinctively into the security of the cave. The tide would not begin to rise until daylight fell, and surely by then the mist would have lifted enough for her to find her way back to the teahouse. Until then, however, she was marooned.

She gazed at the thick misty curtain that shut her into the cave, and she wondered if Ryk van Helden would give her a thought. She doubted it, and after a while she resumed her search for the ring – a hopeless task, but it took her mind off the mist, and the queer whisperings that seemed to come from first one corner, and then another. Rivulets of water began to run down the walls, and the waves churned restlessly out there in the mist-shrouded world.

She began to whistle a tune to keep up her spirits. The dampness was beginning to penetrate her thin clothing, and she wondered uneasily what she would do if the white fog didn't lift. The tide line ended a yard or so from the cave, so the big waves would not wash in. All the same it would be wretchedly cold if she had to spend the night here – eerie as well.

She stood and stared at the unmoving mist, and a chilliness crept over her skin. To be alone in a fog was to feel like the last soul on earth, and she thought of the lamplit *salon* at the palace, with the brocade curtains pulled to shut out the mist, and the tea being poured from a lacquered pot.

Her longing for a cup of hot sweet tea was almost more than she could bear, and she began to pace back and forth in an effort to keep up her circulation. A thread of uneasiness kept tightening inside her. Alone, cut off, clad in thin clothing, she would be lucky if she survived the night!

And it was at that moment, with the shadows deepening and her spirits at a low ebb, that she glanced down and caught a faint glimmer near one of her sandalled feet. She bent down eagerly, and a little cry of wonderment escaped her. It was her mother's ring!

It lay small and slightly dulled in the palm of her hand, and then her fingers clenched over it. 'Be my talisman,' she whispered. 'Make the mist roll away, so I shan't have to stay here – all alone.'

The voice of the incoming sea answered, and the cave

captured the sound as though in a giant shell. The waves swelled and crashed upon the rocks, and the mist was blown into the cave by the rising sea-wind.

Temple tried not to listen as she polished the ring on her trews and slipped it back on her finger. The pearl within the circle of garnets gleamed like a tear . . . pearls were said to bring bad luck, but it was just an old fable and had nothing to do with her present predicament. All the morning there had been a mist over the sea. It had still been hanging about during her swim, so she had no one to blame but herself for lingering here instead of going home to the teahouse.

Only Mei had known that she was going for a swim on her own, and Temple felt cold to the bone as she remembered the way the girl had looked at her on her return from the palace. Mei would not tell anyone that she was missing . . . Ryk least of all!

A long time seemed to pass, and the cave was deep in shadow, and the sea was lashing like an animal in the thick net of mist, when all at once Temple heard voices – real voices, those of men, calling her name. 'Tem-pel! Nona Lane . . . Tem-pel!'

Torches flared through the mist, live flame leaping in the darkness.

'*Meisje.*' That resonant voice rang out above the others. 'Temple, are you here? *Temple!*'

'Ryk!' his name broke from her. She went running from the cave, into the misty ring of light made by the flaring torches. Hands caught at her, a violence in them. Her relief at seeing other human beings was so acute that all she could do was bury her face in a thick jersey over a broad chest and tremble like a leaf – something she had always sworn she would never do in Ryk van Helden's presence.

'We thought you might have walked into the sea!' His voice was as rough as his hands. The smell of sea

114

mist was on him, and when at last she raised her face it was so pale in the torchlight that her mouth looked bruised. She looked about her and saw that he had brought about a dozen men from the village to help look for her. She saw the glint of their teeth. Their kindly hands patted her. Only Ryk's hands were angry, bruising.

He shook her. 'What a foolish thing to do, to linger here on the beach with a mist coming inland from the sea! Did common sense not warn you that it would thicken?'

'Th-there's no need to blister my ears off.' Her teeth chattered, half from cold, half from nervous reaction and the blessed relief of being found. 'I-I'm so c-cold—'

He said something to one of the men, and the next moment she was wrapped in a woolly blanket, and Ryk was pouring something that steamed into the cup of a flask. 'Here you are!' She took the cup and drank the hot, sweet, whisky-laced tea in thirsty gulps. It raced through her, bringing warmth back into her body.

'Thank you.' She managed a shaky smile as she cuddled down into the blanket. 'I was plucking up the courage to spend the night in the cave. What made you – I mean, how did you know I was caught out in the mist?'

'It occurred to me that you might have decided to swim alone, and enquiries for you at the teahouse confirmed my suspicions. You really are an irresponsible *kind*, and it would not have surprised me if you had ventured out into the mist and found yourself in the sea!'

'I – I've a bit more sense than that,' she protested, and she could hardly believe from his tone of voice that he had felt anxious about her. It would, she supposed, have been inconvenient if he had found himself without a secretary on Monday morning!

'*Wanita takut?*' One of the men thrust his face close to her and grinned like a devil. '*Sétan mist. Djahat.*'

Temple glanced helplessly at Ryk, too confused to be

115

able to understand what the man was saying.

'He asks if you were afraid. This is a devil mist – bad.' Ryk shot his fierce smile at the villager. He spoke rapidly in the tongue of the island, and the other man spread his hands significantly.

'What did you say to him?' Temple asked.

'That you are like a child and see danger in trifles, and no danger where it really exists.'

'Thank you!'

'You are very welcome.'

'A – a stone could be moved to sympathy quicker than you!'

'I daresay.' He turned and spoke to the men, and she thought how strange and unreal everything was, with the flames of the torches burning through the mist and showing the gleam of dark eyes, the thrust of cheekbones, the lips that moved and made words she could not understand fully.

'Come!'

Her breath caught in her throat as she was swept up in Ryk's arms and she felt the rough, sea-misted wool of his sweater against her cheek. 'I – I can walk,' she protested.

'In a blanket, with half-numbed legs?' His voice sank down until it was against her ear. 'Think of me as a Dutch bolster,' he said mockingly.

He looked like a Dutch pirate, black-clad, the eye-patch outlined in the flame-lit denseness. A pirate carrying her off along a fog-bound beach, surrounded by his crew!

At one point she heard the surge of the sea, overwhelming and fearful, and Ryk's arms drew her into the hard hollow of his shoulder. The strange torchlight procession wended its slow, careful way through the black mist, and Temple felt the beat of her heart in confusion with Ryk's, and a laughing remark was carried to her on the sea-wind. *'Tuan besar kuat.'* The master was strong . . . he had to be, for he was about to carry her up the cliffs!

'Ini!' The leader of the procession had found the path.

'He must have eyes like a cat,' Temple murmured, and heard with faint surprise the drowsy note in her voice. She was tired, but she mustn't fall asleep on Ryk. . . .

'He's a hunter, *memburi itu*. Such men have the sight of a tiger.'

Her cheek pressed with sudden closeness to the rough wool, the warmth, the hard, living beat of the heart inside this man. Too many things had hurt him and it was no longer easy for him to be tender. But all the same he had got together a search party and he and his men had dared the hazard of the cliffs in the fog in order to find her. He had not left her to face a night alone in a cold, damp, fog-bound cave.

She was grateful. She wanted to tell him so . . . she glanced up, but his words cut across hers. 'Put your arms about my neck and hold on tightly,' he ordered.

She did as she was told, and it was as if in a dream that she felt herself carried up the cliff path. Her head felt heavy and it kept nodding against his shoulder. Nothing was real any more, but the hard warmth and sinew to which she clung. . . .

She awoke with a start as light blazed around her. She felt dazed, and the strong arms were letting go of her. 'Yes, *tuan*,' out of the confusion a face came close and dark eyes stared into hers. 'I will put *mem* to bed and see she has warm drink.'

'No—' Temple struggled to sit up, but a strong hand eased her back against the cushions of a long chair. 'You will be all right with Mei.' The deep voice came to her in waves. 'You are out of the cave, *meisje*. Safe at the teahouse.'

Safe? She fought the waves of fatigue, the drowning lethargy, the mist that had got into her mind and was clouding her senses. 'I'm not safe – here,' she wanted to say. 'Each time you speak to me, look at me, touch me, drag me out of danger, you put a little more hate into Mei's eyes. Can't you see? Oh, can't you *see*?'

'I – I don't want to stay here—' the words broke from her.

'Then you must ask Alan to take you away.' The voice was distant, cold. 'He will soon be flying back to the island.'

She struggled to open her eyes, but Ryk was gone and it was too late to say that it wasn't the island she wished to leave. The *chik* clattered, and she closed her eyes again so that Mei would not see the weary tears in them.

CHAPTER TEN

In the week that followed Temple visited the bamboo hospital whenever she had some time to spare, for she found Tofan very amusing. He was now allowed out of bed, and Khun Lan found him a bit of a handful and was grateful to Temple for keeping the boy occupied for an hour or two.

She learned from Khun Lan that the headman's wife had not yet given birth to her child and that the *doktor* hoped to return in time for the event.

It would be quite an event, Khun Lan added with his rather grave smile. If the child was a boy, then the festival lanterns would be brought out and the islanders would celebrate with a feast and dancing.

'If the birth coincides with the Feast of the Full Moon,' Khun Lan spread his slender hands, 'then, *nang-sau*, you will see a spectacle that you will remember always.'

He told her about the Dance of the Dragon. The Dragon was a sea-god and he would be honoured, and propitiated, at the full of the new moon, so that the islanders would get their share of good fishing in the coming months. It was a rather fierce dance-drama, and the best male dancer in the village would be called upon to perform it.

Khun Lan bent rather low over the tea-bowls as he poured Temple a second helping of island tea. She could not see his eyes as he added that there would also be dancing by the girls of the village. They were trained from small children in the art, and he knew of one girl who was so graceful that she made the breeze-blown casuarina look clumsy.

Temple sipped her tea and ate a rice cake, and she wondered who the girl was whom the rather shy and charming Khun Lan admired. She would have liked to ask if he referred to Madu – which meant honey – the rather pretty girl who worked as a nurse at the hospital, but he changed the subject abruptly.

There was to be a shadow-play in the village the following evening and he wondered if Temple would like to see it.

'Very much,' she smiled, and guessed that if he had an evening off from the hospital, then Madu would be on duty, which would make it impossible for her to see the *wayang,* a puppet drama in which the scenes of the play were enacted from behind a screen, on which they cast their shadows. Several times Temple had heard the strange music of these plays echoing up the valley, and she had sat at a window of the teahouse and listened in fascination.

'Always the *wayang* begins late,' Khun Lan escorted her through a side door into the compound of the hospital. 'Will the *nangsau* be as good as to meet me here? I am on duty until eight o'clock.'

'You do a splendid job, Khun Lan.'

He bowed and accepted the compliment with grace. 'I could not work for a more industrious man than the *tuan,*' he murmured.

'Dr. Kinraid is certainly a man of skill and charm,' she agreed.

'Yes, indeed.' Khun Lan's eyes held a subtle smile. 'But I referred to the Mijnheer. He is the one in authority, to whom even the headman bows his head.'

She looked rather sharply at Khun Lan, for once again she detected a note of hostility in his voice. 'You mean, Khun Lan, that it was he who brought you here to work?'

'The skills which the *tuan* requires are not always to be

found on the island.' The gaze of the young Siamese brooded on the palm fronds outlined against the rose and saffron sky. 'The people of Bayanura are a little pagan and content to remain that way, so the *pembesar* hires from other more advanced places the medical aid which keeps his workers fit.'

'Are you not happy on the island?' Temple asked in surprise.

'Happiness is but a moment snatched. A smile that warms, and then leaves a coolness.' Khun Lan bowed and was again in retreat from the curiosity in Temple's eyes. '*Selamat malam, Nona* Lane.'

'*Selamat tinggal,* Khun Lan.'

She made her way through the village, for she wanted to call in at the store for a few things. The saffron and rose of the evening sky were deepening as she emerged with purchases. A woman passed carrying her baby in a hip-sling, and she smiled and greeted Temple who felt warmed and almost a part of the life here as she strolled past the houses on their raised platforms, shaggily thatched and with their sides open to admit the cool evening breezes.

She smelled the pungent rice curries, and the chicken cooked in leaves with ginger. There were banana clumps where children played, and papaya trees curved as if from the weight of their clustering fruits.

The thatching of the houses seemed to burn as the sky flamed gold and crimson. A man sang lazily, for the working day was almost over and he could enjoy being waited on like a lord by his smiling, dark-eyed wife.

Temple smiled to herself and was unaware as she stood a moment, gazing back at the village, that her eyes were huge and wistful. A really happy family life was something she had never known, and at times like these such a longing for it caught at her heart. The laughter of children, the smell of cooking food, the chatter of women at their household tasks, evoked a cosy picture that did not await her at the teahouse.

She turned to proceed on her way, and then suddenly she stood still as she caught sight of a tall, solitary figure standing beneath a mango tree. The cicadas chirred and a great moth fluttered by, and she saw that the path led out of the tea plantations, where the tea bushes stood in compact rows and filled the air with the scent of their big leaves. Some of the workers chanted as they wended their way home along another path.

Temple stood taut . . . as if in the path of a tiger.

'*Dag!*' He rested lazily against the tree looking rough-haired, big and healthily spent. His light khaki shirt clung to the muscles of his chest . . . not the kind of man you could ever imagine in a city suit.

He flicked a glance over her cream sleeveless dress, with a flutter of scarlet chiffon at her throat. 'You look very cool, *meisje,* as if dipped in ice.'

She couldn't answer him. It was as if he insinuated that she had been at a garden-party while he did all the work!

'It has been a hot day,' as he spoke he moved out from among the trees, and the last of the sunlight turned his hair to a fiery gold. 'I thought of going for a swim – would you care to join me?'

Again she couldn't speak, and he smiled with a faint touch of mockery as he stood and quizzed her, thumbs in the slant pockets of his khaki slacks. 'There will be no mist tonight, only the new moon. Have you ever bathed by moonlight?'

A breeze teased the chiffon at her throat, and she looked away from the deep opening at the throat of his shirt. A few minutes ago she had longed for company, but she had not dreamed of seeking Ryk van Helden's – or of being sought by him. He disturbed her more than ever. Was he exercising his '*droit de Seigneur*'? Or did he need her company because the loneliness of the palace appalled him?

The sun smouldered out of sight as she looked at him; the path out of the tea valley filled with deep violet shadow. She met that disconcerting light and dark glance of his, and the grey of his eye was lonesome, like the sea far out.

'I – I should have to go to the teahouse for my bathing things,' she said.

'Borrow a sarong from one of the women,' he gestured at the village. 'Come!' He took her by the wrist and she hurried to keep up with him. He paused below the steps of one of the *atap* houses and called a name. A slender boy ran out and Ryk spoke to him. The boy grinned and went inside the house again, and next time a woman appeared.

Temple gathered from the exchange of words that the *tuan* was welcome to the entire contents of the humble house. He laughed and shook his head, and assured the *njonja* that all he wished for was a wrap-around for the *wanita* to swim in.

A sly smile was cast in Temple's direction, and almost at once a flowered sarong was produced.

'I dare not wear it!' Temple gasped.

'I am sure you will be more cautious this time.' Ryk spoke drily. 'Thank the *njonja* in her own dialect. It will give her great pleasure.'

'*Terima kasih banjak,*' Temple said shyly.

The woman bowed over her hands, placed in the graceful attitude of prayer. Her eyes sparkled inquisitively, and Temple knew that she stood on her veranda and watched as they made their way out of the village Ryk paused beside a mango tree and as he retrieved a leather satchel from a branch, he cast a rather wicked smile at Temple.

'A bottle of wine, a seedcake, and my bathing trunks,' he drawled.

'All arranged, I see,' she rejoined.

'All but the company.'

She accepted this, for she couldn't imagine him way-laying her on purpose.

'Even I am capable of giving way to impulse,' he said, as he swung the satchel over his shoulder. 'You looked a little lonely, so I thought I would ask you to join me.'

'I thought you too armoured, too self-controlled to have impulses, *meneer*. What a discovery!'

A parakeet squawked on a branch as they made their way through the dusky forest towards the cliffs and the beach below. Gibbons swung and chattered overhead, and Temple was aware of their bright little eyes through the meshes of vine that bound the trees and hung them with great musky trumpet-flowers.

A forest at sundown, and at dawn, gave back to one a feeling of the world untouched, Temple thought. Man and woman were given paradise to dwell in, and yet they had to listen to the voice of discord.

Her eyes dwelt on Ryk as he paused upon the path to brush aside something with his arm. She guessed it to be one of those huge webs, often occupied by something dark, legged, and creepy. She walked towards Ryk, and the many leaves rustled and things moved unseen, and she wanted – oh, she didn't know what she wanted, not with Ryk.

He might unbend to ask her to go swimming with him, but she did not feel at ease with him. She was on the de-fensive, and friendship was based on a relaxation of the barriers and restraints that made people feel so alone; so locked up within themselves.

With Ryk she was still aware of being alone. To him she was a visitor to the island, an employee who had to be noticed now and again. He never noticed her as a woman. Perhaps he still carried in his mind a picture of her dressed as a boy on the *Egret*.

They emerged on to the cliffs, and they paused to listen to the breaking surf, and to breathe the sea tang in the air. From here they could have counted the stars that burned against the dark violet of the tropical sky.

'It's unbelievable,' she murmured. 'You have lived close to this for many years, *meneer*, but surely its magic must still take your breath away?'

'Magic spells are for young, leggy girls with stars in their eyes,' he said dryly.

She glanced up at him, and there in her large eyes glistened a captive star. 'You think me very young, don't you, *meneer*?'

'You are very young, *meisje*.' He tilted back his head and his profile was outlined strong and ruthless against the starlight. 'Some of us are old at forty.'

'You are not forty!'

'I am fairly close to it. Come, or the tide will be riding high and I might have to come to your rescue again.'

'I'm not a bad swimmer,' she protested. 'Alford has an open-air swimming-pool and I swam regularly through the summer months. My cousins never liked the water. They played tennis at the country club, and were keen on ballroom dancing.'

'You paint me a perfect picture of them, and yourself.' He gave her a helping hand down the steep cliffside path. 'You must not go back there, now you have gained your freedom.'

A light breeze ran its fingers across the back of her neck, and she told herself it was the cause of the cold little shiver than ran through her. They walked across the sands, and the waves broke over the rocks, and the palm trees brooded along the shore.

'There is your cave,' Ryk pointed it out. 'What were you doing in there on Sunday? You have not told me.'

'I was looking for my ring.' The garnets shone darkly as she showed him her hand. 'It slipped off and I – I couldn't bear the thought of losing it.'

'I see.' His leather satchel thumped to the sands. 'Go and put on your sarong. I will change by those rocks.'

After she had undressed and fastened the sarong around her, she took off her ring and put it away in her purse. She wasn't taking a second chance on losing it!

She stepped out of the cave and was at once aware, as she caught sight of Ryk at the water's edge, of her bare shoulders and slim bare legs below the short hem of the sarong. A momentary panic shook her, for an almond-shell of a moon had broken through the palm fronds and its light gleamed down on the wide-shouldered, lean, hard body of Ryk. He blended with the rocks and the surge of the waves. His hair was tousled, white-gold in the moonlight as he swung round and watched Temple approach him bare-footed across the sands.

He met her half-way and looked her over in the sarong. 'It will come off again in the water if you wear it like that.' His teeth gleamed in a half smile. 'Fasten it over your left shoulder – look, let me show you.'

She felt his touch and could not prevent herself from backing away from him. His glance narrowed. 'Do you find me sinister to look at?' he demanded.

'No.' She took a breath of the sweet, salty air. 'No, it isn't that—'

'I think, Temple Lane, that you need to be soundly kissed. It would help you to be less self-conscious.' He took firm hold of her bare shoulders, and she shuddered, weak with a terrible fear of him. She felt him bend over her, but all he did, impassive-faced as a monument, was to unfasten the sarong from between her shoulder-blades and refastened it over her shoulder.

'Now your modesty is safeguarded.' The look he gave her was mercilessly mocking. 'You might be taken for an island girl, but you have better shaped feet.'

'Thanks!' She escaped from him and ran down the

126

beach, the sand between her toes, the surf breaking high to collect her into its embrace. Lovely, tingling, hiding her from Ryk! She struck out, lifted like flowered flotsam on the waves. Exhilarating, dangerous, with Ryk swimming through the waves, his hand upon her foot, her leg, her waist.

'*Don't!*' She laughed and slipped free of him, and in the pagan moonlight they swam until the waves began to take her breath. Then Ryk took her in a hold she could not escape and made her swim back to the beach with him. He held her hand and they raced breathlessly out of reach of the great arcs of water.

She knelt and watched the surging tide, and every inch of her body tingled and glowed.

'Towel!' Ryk tossed it to her, and his wet arm gleamed like polished copper in the moonlight. She wiped the moisture from her arms and legs, and watched him walk up the beach and collect driftwood from above the tideline. He was going to make a fire! They were going to drink the wine and eat seedcake beside the smoky blue flames of a driftwood fire.

She sat and watched the spirals of smoke rise up from the driftwood fire, and felt the warmth on her legs. She and Ryk had dressed, and he looked a little less untamed. A strand of hair lay across his forehead and he lounged at his ease, the moonlight stroking his bold features.

He handed her the mug into which he had poured some of the red wine. '*Drinken op*,' he half teased, and took a swig from the bottle. She sipped her wine, and ate a piece of cake. It tasted good after that tingling swim.

The moon drifted in its half-shell, and the palm fronds creaked as a breeze sighed through them.

'The moon, say the Malayans, is a woman. She is tied by a rope which her lord is always hauling.'

Temple looked at Ryk over the rim of her mug – in

which he probably drank his tea during the day. 'Men like to think they have women on the end of a line, don't they?'

'Do they?' His teeth snapped in a laugh. 'To my way of thinking women are about as easily led as the moon, and it is men who are hauled along in the wake of a primitive spell.'

She gazed into the fire and thought of the way Nick had fallen beneath Lua's spell. Ryk himself was caught and held by a tragic memory.

'Life can make one feel afraid,' she said thoughtfully. 'There are so many mistakes we can make, and some of them can never be put right.'

'What mistake are you regretting?' His gaze flicked her slight figure in the firelight, and dwelt on the hand that wore once again the pearl and garnet ring. 'Are you wishing you had not run away from your erring fiancé?'

She flushed slightly, for he seemed to gibe at what she had felt for Nick, and hoped to find with him at Lumbaya. He seemed to dismiss her as too young, too untried to have felt the full pain of love. It had hurt enough to be disillusioned, and she was suddenly assailed by a need to hurt Ryk.

'We all know that there has never been a romance as deeply felt, as tragic and lasting as your own,' she flashed. 'You dwell on memories, and worship at the shrine you've made of that blue and gold room at the palace. . . .'

Silence followed her words, menacing and filled with the thunder of the surf. She wanted to jump to her feet and run away, for something frightening had invaded his expression and she knew she had gone too far.

He stood the wine bottle in the sand and slowly he towered to his feet. He strode round to her side of the fire and swiftly he took hold of her hand, almost crushing her fingers, digging the garnets and the pearl into her flesh. He jerked her up against him, and the stars were lost, and the moon was hauled out of sight, and there was no-thing – nothing in the world but his mouth on hers, his arms holding her, bruising her against his chest.

Ruthlessly he forced back her head into the cradle of his arm and kissed her without hardly a breath taken be-tween the kisses. Long, hard, searching her facial hol-lows, her soft young throat where her pulse was like a bird trying to escape. 'No – Ryk,' she begged blindly against his hard jaw, but uncaring, hurt and hurting, he found the soft hollows of her shoulder with his hard lips. . . .

Then, with an abruptness that was equally painful, he released her and pushed a strand of hair back from his eyes. His chest rose and fell, his chin was cleft by shadow, and she wanted to weep because he could look and act so cruelly.

'You asked for that,' he bit out. 'It will teach you not to be presumptuous. To take for granted that because you are young and unworldly you can say just what you like.'

'Y-you don't like the truth,' she threw back at him. 'And your own presumption is something to marvel at! You think no one ever loved before, or lay awake at night wanting comfort from someone special. You think I'm too callow to feel like that, about someone who is al-ways going to be out of my reach.'

She turned away from him and looked at the surging sea. She felt so shaken that the ground seemed to heave beneath her feet, and she fought to get her nerves under control. She heard a sizzle as he quenched the fire with the remainder of the wine. It was, somehow, a signifi-cant gesture.

'Come!'

That familiar order, to which she responded frozenly, falling into step beside him as he walked up the beach towards the homeward path. About halfway up a tangle of flowering vine caught at her hair and she brushed it away, wanting not even the touch of a flower at this moment. The moonlight made the flowers look dark, like her lips and her eyes.

All the way through the forest she evaded contact with Ryk, who seemed to know the way as though it were a line upon the palm of his hand.

She smelled the tea that slumbered in the valley, where each day it was plucked from the bushes into baskets and taken to the factory to be withered and to go through the various processes that turned it into a rich dark brew. From storage in bins, it was loaded into tea-chests to be taken off in boats to the mainland.

The forest brooded all around, a deep, velvety nesting place for all kinds of animals – even the tiger upon occasion. He was known to slink down from the mountains, and this was one of the reasons the village houses were built off the ground.

Suddenly there was a swoop of wide, dark wings and something seemed to fly straight towards Temple from among the trees. Her nerves were already on edge and as the winged creature swooped close to her, she gave a little cry and stood petrified, her hands over her face. She had never been so frightened and she trembled as the wings brushed her hair, and then it was gone as suddenly as it had appeared and a pair of hands caught at her and a voice told her roughly that it was only a large type of moth.

'Let me go!' The words broke through the hands she held pressed to her face.

'Don't be foolish—'

'I can't help being what I am! Young and foolish and unused to the things you've always lived with!' She was on the verge of tears and fighting not to give way to them. 'I – if that was a moth, then what do the bats look like?'

'Some are no larger than my thumbnail.' His voice was

a few notes gentler. 'Stop trembling – *dadelijk*. It was not a tiger, after all.'

She drew her hands down from her face and looked at him with eyes from which she had blinked her tears, fiercely. 'You're never afraid, are you, *meneer*? Not of the things of the forest – not even of tigers. It's because you have no feelings any more. You feel nothing, for nobody!'

She brushed past him and hurried along the *laan* to the teahouse. Its lanterns gleamed low along the veranda, and she did not look back as she crossed the compound and mounted the steps. She pushed open the screen door and entered the lounge. Outside in the night the things of the forest croaked and chirred and prowled in the shadows.

Temple sank down suddenly exhausted on to a cane lounger. She felt cold, though the night was warm. She felt the emptiness of the teahouse, but it didn't worry her. She didn't stir for a long while, lost in her thoughts, and yet aware all the time of the throb of a bruise from that savage embrace down on the beach.

CHAPTER ELEVEN

THE shadow-play was to be held in the courtyard of the village temple, and it was something for Temple to look forward to as she sat at the typewriter the following day.

She was well into the diary by now, and had reached the part in which Polyana wrote of the birth of her son. 'Such a bright-eyed child, and Laurens looked so proud when he came to me after the birth and gave me a beautiful pin of jade for my hair – just like the women of the East, who wear such a pin in their hair to proclaim proudly to everyone that they have a son.

'But,' the diary went on, 'my dear Laurens and I were to suffer a terrible blow when Jan was two years old. He suffered a bite from a scorpion and though everything possible was done to try and save his young life, he passed out of our keeping as he had come into it, looking like a fair, small angel. . . .'

Temple felt tears on her lashes, and she glanced up from the diary and her glance dwelt gravely on the archway that let in fretted patterns of sunlight and the bird calls from the palace garden. Her horn-rims added to her look of gravity, and she wore cool blue linen with a white collar. The short sleeves of the dress showed that her slim arms had caught the sunshine.

She sighed and wondered why life held so many tests of courage for people. Poor Polyana, to lose the child she had gone through so much pain to give birth to!

Temple thought of the woman down in the village, Lontah, who was due to have her child at any time. It was a wonderful, yet a lonely and testing time in a woman's life. A culmination of the desires which a certain man awakes, and which his child brings to fulfilment.

The clock chimed on the lacquered cabinet, and Temple saw that it was time for her *breken,* as Ryk van Helden had called it. She arose from the desk and wandered out to the patio, where she sat on the sun-warmed seat at the side of the lotus pond and watched the lovely pink and white flowers of the East floating on their great platter-like leaves.

Ranji brought her a tray on which stood a cup of coffee, several coconut cakes, and slices of delicious chilled mango. 'The *nonya* likes mango, so I bring.' He gave her his golden smile and arranged the tray on the seat beside her.

'*Terima kasih.*' She gestured at the lotus flowers. 'So pretty, Ranji, like doll's cups on outsize saucers.'

'They drift, pink and pale with secrets like a woman in love.' Ranji was looking at the pool, but Temple felt that he was watching her out of the sides of his oblique eyes.

A blue parakeet settled on a nearby branch and cocked his crested head at the tray beside Temple. He had spotted the coconut cakes and any second now he would dare to hop a little closer. She crumbled a cake in readiness. 'Pretty boy,' she said. 'Say pretty, pretty boy.'

Ranji shook his dark-capped head at the English girl who talked to birds and fed them. *Masja Allah.* She should have a man and a home at her age, not a machine to bang with her white hands, and birds to take titbits from them.

'Don't you approve, Ranji?' She laughed up at him and her face had a fey sort of charm which the horn-rims somehow intensified. 'This is how a fruitless fig-tree amuses herself.'

She knew that single women were referred to as such, and she was over twenty and must seem to the men on the island to be withering on the branch.

'The *nonya* makes a joke,' Ranji said solemnly. 'A girl of Bayanura would weep if she had no one to love her.'

133

His slippered feet whispered across the stones of the patio, and then his white-clad figure disappeared inside the palace. Temple drank her coffee and fed the cheeky parakeet with cake crumbs. Others less daring scolded from the trees, and the ballet of the lotus flowers was lovely in the sunlight.

Pink and pale with secret like a woman in love . . . then with a slight gasp Temple glanced round, feeling that she was watched, but there was no one near the moon-flower tree. She must have imagined that someone stood there, still, silent, half lost among the great creamy flowers.

Her nerves were still on edge. She feared to see Ryk after last night, for she would no longer be able to look at him without feeling her body pressed hurtfully close to him, without feeling the crush of his mouth, and breathing the salt-bloom on his brown skin.

She jumped to her feet and startled the parakeet. He squawked and flew off, and she hurried indoors to lose herself in the diary of a ghost. Perhaps Polyana haunted the palace and its gardens, drawn back by the reopening of the pages of her life. Temple did not fear this ancestress of Ryk's. She too had been English, with ways and feelings that seemed strange to the people she had come to live among.

Temple was soon absorbed in her work, and it was some time in the afternoon when Ranji appeared with a sealed envelope on a little round tray. A boy from the village had just delivered the note for *Nona* Lane.

'Thank you, Ranji.' She studied the delicate script on the front of the envelope and did not open it until the door closed quietly behind Ryk's manservant. He had probably asked the boy who had sent it, anyway. These people were as innocently curious as children.

She slit the envelope with the small filigreed *kris* which Ryk kept on his desk, and withdrew the folded note. It was from Khun Lan; he sent profuse apologies to the *nangsau,* for he would be unable to keep his promise to take her to see the *wayang.* A personal matter intervened with his intention to do so, and he hoped she would not think too badly of him.

She was disappointed, and then as she sat toying with the *kris* it occurred to her that there was nothing to stop her from going on her own. She was on nodding terms with quite a few of the villagers, and they wouldn't mind if she sat among them to enjoy one of their fascinating, age-old shadow-plays.

Yes, she would go alone. She had looked forward to the *wayang* all day, and the prospect of a solitary evening at the teahouse did not appeal to her. Mei had taken to slipping away when the evening meal was over and though Temple didn't mind, it had grown disturbing to be alone with her thoughts, and the mysterious noises which surrounded the teahouse at night.

She was covering the typewriter and on the point of departing for the day when a tall figure appeared in the opening of the archway. She tensed at once and felt as if the tip of a lash flicked all her nerves. It was a disconcerting moment, for she had hoped to avoid seeing Ryk.

She could not stand indefinitely with a downcast gaze – like a slave girl. She had to look up and meet Ryk's gaze as he sauntered into the room. As he drew near to the desk where she stood, she backed against the teakwood, a slim, defensive figure in blue, with a white collar framing her pale young throat. Quite unintentionally her fingers closed upon the *kris,* with its sharp and shining blade.

'You don't need to defend yourself,' he said sardonically.

'Oh—' She glanced down at the *kris* and dropped it as if it had stung her. 'I – I'm always toying with it—'

'It looks like a toy, but I believe it could kill.' His

brown fingers flicked through the piled pages of manuscript she had left ready for his inspection. 'You have been working hard, *meisje*.'

'I find the work absorbing, *meneer*.'

'At this rate the diaries will soon be typed out and ready for the publishers. Are you so anxious to get away from the island?'

She met the probe of his keen grey eye. 'I'm not anxious at all, but it's quiet here all day and I'm a fairly quick typist, and apart from that Polyana is such an entertaining writer that I don't find the work in the least tedious.'

'You spoke on Sunday about wanting to go away. I assumed you had grown homesick for city life. For theatres and shops, and your own kind of people.'

'I'd been through a rather shattering experience.' She forced a laugh, and could not mention the strange fears she felt whenever she set foot in the teahouse. If she told him that she wanted to stay elsewhere he might assume that she meant the palace. There was nowhere else for her to stay. All the houses in the villages were occupied, and Khun Lan had a room in the bungalow attached to the hospital. Alan's bungalow!

'You and your men, *meneer*, had just rescued me from a benighted cave down on the beach.'

'I had not forgotten.' He crossed to the lacquered drinks cabinet. 'Will you join me in a sundowner?'

She wanted to refuse, but to do so would make it seem as if she were nervous of being alone with him in the dusk that was creeping into the room.

'A small one,' she said.

He shot her a rather quizzical look, then took squat tankards from a shelf of the cabinet and mixed a couple of planter's punches. The tang of cinnamon drifted to her nostrils, edged with lime as he cut one and squeezed it into the drinks. He replaced the little silver spice box, and turned to her with the tankards in his hands.

'A hard day's work deserves a planter's punch.' He came to her and gave her one of the tankards. They were Dutch and painted with windmills and girls with Delft-blue eyes gathering armfuls of tulips.

'The planters of long ago brought such tankards with them to remind them of home.' He smiled briefly. 'Idealistic scenes, but then the men who leave their homeland to open up industries in other lands are often idealistic.'

She sipped her spicy drink, while the dusk deepened and the scents of the garden stole in through the archway. A great cluster of jessamine had broken into bloom all down one side of the arch, and now the sun had gone down in the valley, the flowers were opening to the velvety touch of night. Ryk touched a lamp and the dusk was broken by golden shadows. The lamplight touched his face, with its thrusting bones bred from strength, adventure, and a dash of ruthlessness.

Though she saw all this in his face, she knew that he too had his ideals. Marta alone had lived up to them.

His hand touched the scarlet clogs that always stood on a deep sill between the windows. They were faded from age, and smooth as silk.

'Have you ever been tempted to try them on?' he asked.

'Once or twice,' she admitted.

'You have a small foot, *meisje*. They should fit you.'

'Do you mean you want me to try them on?'

'It would amuse me.'

She looked at him over the rim of her tankard, and his mood baffled her. Had he forgotten so completely those kisses he had forced upon her, down on the beach? Had it not hurt him – just a little – to be called heartless?

'Put them on.' He handed her the clogs and his smile was faintly mocking. 'Those doll's feet of yours should

137

slip into them quite easily.'

'I wonder what you did for entertainment when I was not here to amuse you?' Her hazel eyes caught the lamplight as she looked at him and took the clogs from his hand.

'I wonder,' he mocked lightly.

She bent her head and slipped her feet out of her sandals and into the scarlet clogs. Kitpup had slipped like a tawny shadow into the room and he came bounding over to Temple and she gave a breathless laugh as she felt his tongue tickling her instep. 'You had your pets, of course, *meneer*,' and there came into her mind an image of Mei, slipping silently through the garden to him, *melati* flowers in her dark hair.

She straightened up and attempted to walk in the clogs. She stumbled and had to clutch at something for support – Ryk's left arm, muscular and warm!

'They must have hurt cruelly to walk in,' she gasped.

'There are country places in Holland where women still wear them about the yards of their farms,' he said. 'You have the pampered feet of a city girl.'

'Alford wasn't all that vivacious and gay,' she rejoined. 'There were three cinemas, a repertory theatre, a Chinese restaurant, and two supermarkets – not forgetting the launderette!'

His laughter sounded soft and dangerous above her head. 'No matter how hard we try, *meisje*, we will always have fireworks.'

'I don't consider that you try to be anything but mocking and superior.' She attempted to walk again in the clogs and as they clattered across the teakwood floor, the tiger-cub came bounding at her heels, growling playfully and clutching her around the ankles. She nearly fell over, and once again Ryk was there to catch hold of her.

'You are obstinate,' his hands pressed into her waist,

'and very British.'

'You are very Dutch,' she threw back at him. 'Like a stone wall—'

'You think so, eh?' He pulled her against him and she felt she would die if he now assumed that he could kiss her wherever there was no tea planting to do and he felt bored.

'Let me go!' She lifted a hand and thrust it wildly against his jaw. 'I'm not one of your little distractions, one of your little slave girls who come running at a snap of your fingers!'

At once it was as if lightning played around them; as if storm came in through the archway and filled the room with its electricity. 'What do you mean?' He spoke quietly enough, but underneath ran a thread of steel, and steel was in his fingers as they almost met around her waist. He could have broken her in half and tossed aside the pieces . . . that was how it felt!

'Y-you know what I mean.' His chin was like rock beneath her hand, and the hammer of his heart was confused with hers. 'I'm not a child that I don't know – I learned too well at Lumbaya that men have a different attitude to – to love.'

'Love? You have not the conception of a week-old infant of what it feels like to love someone.' His face was dangerous and hard. 'You ran away from that young man at Lumbaya because he hurt your pride. You will be sure to run away when your heart becomes in danger of being taken. It hurts even more to lose your heart to someone.'

'No doubt it does,' she said defensively. 'If that someone doesn't want it.'

The tiger-cub purred with happy indifference and wound his plump body in and out of their legs. Ryk let her go, and yet the pressure of his hands lingered, held her without any holding as she removed the clogs and stepped into her sandals.

'I must be getting home to the teahouse,' she said. She did not mention the *wayang* and that she intended to go and see it. She picked up her purse and made sure her hand torch was in it. 'Will that be all, *meneer*?'

He laughed and finished his drink. '*Ja, mijn secreta-resse.*'

'Goodnight.' She walked quickly out of the archway and the jessamine brushed her shoulder and filled her nostrils with their scent.

The *laan* was dark with the shadows of trees; they shut out the moon, and the beam of her torch moved ahead of her like an eye. The tropical night was filled with croaks and chirrings and the flutterings of restless birds, but she was hardly aware of them. It was not the thousand-eyed night from which she hurried.

Lanterns cast an unreal glow over the courtyard of the temple; stone gods and miniature dragons lurked among the trailing vines and the rain-trees. Strange trees, whose leaves curled up and collected moisture through the night, to be released as rain as soon as the morning sun touched the leaves and opened them.

Half concealed by a fan palm, Temple watched the weaving of illusion and magic with the use of puppets. The red shawl of Indian silk was held lightly about her, and the strange wail of a flute, the intentness of everyone as they watched the shadow princess being wooed by the hero in the disguise of a demon, was exciting and alien.

The half moon added to the sense of mystery, outlining the curved roofs of the old temple, half revealing the stone idols and the living people who sat almost in imitation of them, only their jaws working as they chewed betel nut, and dragon nut, a small fruit like nutty grapes.

Temple had been noticed by members of the audience as she had slipped in to join them. Dark eyes had looked at her intently, and then that strange Asian veil had been lowered and no one had spoken. She supposed it was because she was without a male companion.

The shadow-plays were rambling and absorbing, and it was often quite late before the puppeteers and the audience grew tired and brought the show to an end. Temple had no intention of staying to the end. The moon was up and she had her hand torch, but it would still be a long walk home – alone.

She slipped out from the *wayang* as cymbals clanged and a battle raged behind the shadow screen. The rest of the *kampong* was quiet enough, and a few lights glimmered behind the bamboo blinds that had been lowered for the night. A pig grunted from beneath the platform of one of the *atap* houses, and she was passing the bamboo hospital when a figure darted down the steps and almost knocked her off her feet.

She flung up the light of her torch, defensively, and the beam shone on the distressed face of a young man. She recognized him as Guntur, the handsome brother-in-law of the village headman. He was also one of Ryk's foremen, and she knew that he spoke a smattering of English.

'Guntur, what is wrong?'

'*Nona* Lane!' He hesitated as he was about to plunge across the *kampong*. 'I look for Khun Lan, but cannot find him. My sister Lontah will die without a *dokter*—'

'What of Madu?' Temple mentioned the nurse at the hospital.

'A child is very sick—' By the light of the torch Guntur's eyes were filled with pain, and he was about to plunge on his way to the headman's house when Temple caught at his arm.

'Perhaps I can be of help?' The words were out before

141

she had fully considered them. What, after all, did she know about helping a woman in labour – bad labour from the look of fear in Guntur's eyes?

'You are nurse?' he asked eagerly.

'No, but I am a woman and I may be able to help.'

'Then come!' He clutched at her hand and she hastened with him in the direction of the headman's residence. Wooden steps led up to the veranda of the shaggily roofed house, which was built on pillars of wood. The light of oil-lamps glimmered behind the split-bamboo curtain which Guntur lifted aside so that Temple might enter the one long room in which the family resided.

A man and an elderly woman turned from the low bedside, and their enquiring glances flashed over Temple. Guntur broke into a rapid explanation. Temple had no idea what he told them, but Lontah's husband evidently assumed that she was as proficient as Khun Lan, for he made way for her at the bedside and gave her a look that pleaded with her to relieve his wife of her suffering.

The perspiration was thick on Lontah's face, it clung to her long eyelashes and beaded her upper lip. She lay on a woven bamboo mat and had a single pillow for her head. Her fingernails had raked the bamboo in her pain, and now she lay looking at Temple with the large eyes of a distressed doe.

Her husband spoke to her and she gave him the travesty of a smile, then as another spasm tore through her body, she cried out incoherently.

'*Njeri itu tidak tertahan.*' Tears gushed from the headman's eyes and down his face, and he gave Temple a look she would never forget. Lontah was his beloved wife and if he lost her the day would go as black as the night. The pain she suffered was not to be borne, and Temple must do something!

Temple knew instinctively that the birth was not going

right. Alan Kinraid had said that Lontah would have a bad time, and Temple wished that a prayer might bring him right this minute, calm and assured and equipped with the knowledge to help Lontah to the utmost.

'*Saja lelah*,' Lontah whispered. She was tired and it was a bad sign. She must fight, and someone was needed who would see to it that she did fight.

Temple turned to Guntur. 'You must fetch Tuan van Helden,' she said firmly. 'Go quickly – very, very quickly.'

The split bamboo clattered behind him, and Temple made the grandmother understand that she wanted a bowl of cool water and a cloth to bathe Lontah's face. The headman seemed incapable of doing anything but kneel by the bedside and watch his wife's face for one of those wrenching, distorting spasms that filled her eyes with a dark despair.

Lontah was almost forty. To give her *suami* a son in their maturity would be the blessing of her life, but the terrible pain was exhausting her, taking all her strength, and she knew it to be the pain of her inability to bring the child into the light.

Temple bathed off the perspiration as it came, and the old woman began to chant to herself. She was saying a prayer for the birth of the *tjutju*, and the lamplight cast her in the shape of a wizened idol, the veined old hands clasped together, the smoke of the lamps mingling with the odour of pain and sweat.

Temple was only half aware of her own prayer – that Ryk come soon and bring with him the strength that was seeping out of Lontah. The vigour that would not allow tea or tobacco plans to wither on the stem.

At last footsteps pounded on the wooden steps outside. She heard the long, decisive strides. The bamboo curtain was thrust aside, and the tall shadow loomed all the way up the walls of the lamplit room.

'Now you are a midwife, *ja*?' He sounded angry, exasperated, even a little concerned. Temple turned her head to look at him, and her hand took the bite of Lontah's fingers as pain racked and tore and arched the body in which the child had bridged.

'Help her!' Temple begged. 'There's no one else with your determination – and this is the life of a woman and a baby – and you said you had to be the doctor when Alan was not here—'

'Calm down, *meisje*.' His hand was on her shoulder as he spoke to Lontah's husband, then he gazed down long and searchingly at Lontah. 'It must be a lazy boy.' A brief smile touched his mouth. 'A young elephant, eh?'

Lontah's eyes held the faintest shadow of a responsive smile as she gazed up at Ryk. '*Baji Gadjah*,' she gasped.

Baby elephant!

Temple caught her breath and wanted to cry with relief at the feeling of hope and invigoration which Ryk had brought into the *atap* house with him. There was no one – no one in the world quite like him.

'Temple,' his fingers dug gently into the bones of her shoulder, 'I am going to carry Lontah over to the hospital, where she can be put into a proper bed. Guntur tells me that Khun Lan is not to be found, and that the nurse is busy with a very sick child, *ja*? Then we must do what we can to help, and the good *Tuhan* help both of us if we bungle this.'

Temple looked at him, not fully comprehending.

'We are breaking *adat*,' he said grimly. 'Custom. If Lontah dies, and her child with her, the blame will then be ours and not that of the gods with their faces turned away.'

'Ryk—' Now she realized what she had done. She had placed upon him a burden that Alan Kinraid, with all his medical skill, might have found himself unable to deal with. In that case it would have been accepted that the *dokter* had done all he could for his patient, but Ryk was not a doctor!

'Come, we have work to do!' He swung round to Guntur and told him to run across to the hospital for a blanket. '*Meisje,* you go with him. See there is a bed ready for Lontah.'

It was cool outside in the night. A wind rustled through the palm trees, and people stood on their latticed verandas, watching silently as she and Guntur came from the headman's house and made for the hospital. They had divined what was going on, and somewhere a leather drum was being softly and rhythmically pounded. It echoed the beat of Temple's heart, intensified her awareness that this island and its people were essentially pagan.

CHAPTER TWELVE

THERE was a patter as of rain as the leaves of the rain-trees unfurled at the first touch of the morning sun.

Suddenly a whimper broke from the child that had come into the world as if lifeless, and Temple could feel herself holding her breath as Ryk breathed once again into the tiny mouth. This time the baby stirred and then the small chest began to flutter and to take on the rhythm of natural breathing.

'Cry, little one,' Ryk coaxed softly, his great hand moving the small limbs and caressing the velvety back and chest. 'Come, a lusty yell that your mother will hear.'

Temple bent over Lontah, who lay so still, her long lashes unmoving on her pain-drawn cheeks. She seemed to have gone too far away to hear anything any more.

'Cry, *baji*.'

And then – surely the loveliest, most primeval sound in the world – the first cry broke from Lontah's son. Her husband stiffened as if struck through the heart, and as a lustier cry broke from the baby his mother began to open her heavy eyes. Great dark eyes that filled with wonderment as the sun struck into the cubicle and lit the hair of the man who held her child.

'*Selamat*.' Ryk placed the child carefully beside her in the bed, and tired though she was Lontah managed to encircle her son with her arm. She smiled and looked eloquently at her husband. He nodded as if he found it too difficult to speak. His elderly mother – who had watched with such dangerous eyes as Ryk had given her son's baby the kiss of life – now caught at Ryk's hand and pressed her forehead to the back of it.

'*Sjukur*,' she said, thanking God. '*Terima kasih banjak, tuan. Terima kasih*,' she added, thanking Ryk.

He replied to her in her own dialect, using the term *nénék*, grandmother. She smiled all over her wrinkled face, and then went to the bedside to gaze at the baby in the circle of Lontah's arm. Ryk's gaze captured Temple's across the cubicle. He made a slight movement with his hand, and she followed him quietly out into the ward and to a door that led outside.

They strolled across the compound and paused beneath a palm tree. Ryk leaned against the tree, lit a cheroot and blew a luxurious cloud of smoke. Temple stretched lazily and felt the warm sun on her skin. Everything was so alive this morning, the colours, the atmosphere, the very air she breathed.

'Lontah has a fine baby,' she murmured, a husky catch in her voice which she could not keep out. 'Thanks to you, *meneer*.'

He quizzed her through his cheroot smoke, and his golden bristles gleamed in a shaft of sunlight through the palm leaves. His hair was damp and tousled, yet still there was a splendour about the man, an affinity with nature, an instinct for tackling problems that other men would have reeled away from. She thought of him with Lontah, and saw the deep, small wounds in his hands where she had clutched at him ... it was then that her child had turned again and in a final spasm of pain had been born. He had seemed lifeless, and even as the grandmother had wailed, Ryk had taken him, wiped him, and breathed life into his small body.

'Make no mistake, *Meisje*.' Ryk spoke rather grimly, and there was a sudden hard set to his jaw. 'I am not a doctor, and last night's drama was not one I would choose to experience again. Khun Lan should have been available in Alan's absence.'

'He was off duty.' She plucked a small wild orchid from

147

a crevice in the palm trunk. 'He invited me to go and see the *wayang* with him, then he sent me a note to say that a personal matter had cropped up and he couldn't take me.'

'You attended the *wayang* alone, eh?'

'I enjoyed it—'

'I don't suppose you understood half of it.'

'Enough to be fascinated. It was rather late when I left, and it was then I bumped into Guntur and offered – well, I thought I could do something to help.'

'The sun would not be shining so brightly, nor would the birds sound so rapturous to you if – if things had gone wrong.' He dropped his cheroot butt to the ground and the down-grinding of his heel upon it was significant.

Temple's heart gave an odd little twist as she looked at him, for not once until now had he betrayed any sign of nerves. Now it had to be remembered that he was used to handling accidents at the tea factory, sometimes a case of snake-bite in the valley, or some other mishap, but last night was the first time he had dealt with a protracted labour, a birth, and the succouring of a newborn infant. Now she saw how tired he looked.

'I need a cool shower, a shave, and a large breakfast,' he said. 'Wait while I go and have a few words with the nurse, then come back to the palace and join me in some kidneys and bacon.'

While he was gone she played idly with the wild orchid, and watched the people of the *kampong* at their morning tasks. A woman was shaking the family sleeping-mats and rolling them deftly. Others were going off to a stream with bundles of laundry on their heads, and a girl was singing as she soaped her small daughter and stood her in a bucket to rinse off the suds.

There was an atmosphere of gaiety in the air. They knew, every one of them, that the headman had a son – forgotten were their suspicions of last night. They flashed their teeth in smiles as Ryk escorted Temple from the village, and suddenly one of them ran across to Temple and handed her a basket of fruit – fingers of gold, papayas, and lotus cones.

'Thank you,' Temple forgot the local words in her confusion. 'Thank you very much.'

'*Nona beruntung.*' The woman bowed low, then retreated with grace in her wrap-around of many colours.

'She says you bring luck to the village,' Ryk translated.

'Do I?' Temple held the basket as though it contained eggs of gold. 'Anyway, it gives one a nice feeling to be thought a luck-bringer.'

He took one of the golden bananas, peeled it and ate the fruit hungrily. 'Do you mind if I share your *tandamata*?'

'You deserve to, *meneer*. Have another.'

He accepted the invitation, while she peeled a lotus cone and ate the fruit of paradise.

Several days passed and all went well with Lontah and her son. When the sound of an aeroplane engine purred over the island at the weekend, Temple glanced up from her typewriter and a smile touched her lips. Alan was circling the runway for a landing, and with luck his visit would be a relaxing one with Lontah out of danger, and the child at the hospital rapidly improving.

She had eaten her evening meal and was curled up with a book when footsteps sounded on the veranda of the teahouse. She sat up and patted her hair, and was ready with a welcoming smile when Alan pushed open the screen door and entered the lounge. He wore white ducks and a gaily printed shirt, and his lopsided smile was good to see.

'Hullo there!' He drew her up out of the cane lounger and just stood looking at her. 'How's the midwifery going?'

'So you've heard?' She laughed and it was amazing that she felt less shyness with this man than with Ryk van Helden. 'Lontah and *meneer* did most of the work. I stood by and offered encouragement.'

'I am sure you were a great help.' He grinned and flicked a look over her. 'You're looking well, Temple. A touch of the sun suits you.'

'I could never raise a tan in England, not even when we had a good summer.' She pulled her hands free of his. 'Can I offer you a drink, Doctor?'

'We agreed to an exchange of first names,' he chided her. 'I'd go for something slim and cool.'

She caught the note of meaning in his voice, and went quickly to the side table on which stood several bottles. Ranji had brought them from the palace the other day, with *meneer*'s compliments. Lime and gin. Whisky and soda-water. Rum and lemon.

'We'll need some ice,' she said to Alan, and left him to make himself comfortable while she went out to the kitchen to fetch some ice from the small refrigerator which ran on kerosene. Mei was just coming in through the back door, and for a moment the kitchen was filled with the chirrings from outside. Mei never said where she had been and who the man was whom she met, and Temple always shied away from asking.

She felt the other girl following her with her eyes as she went from the ice-box to the table and opened a tin of cheese biscuits. 'Dr. Kinraid has called in for a drink,' she said.

'Would *mem* like me to bring in more food?'

'No.' Temple shook the circular biscuits on to a plate. 'I expect the doctor has dined at the palace.'

'Oh, yes,' said Mei, and when Temple glanced up the small red mouth was mocking, and a heavy silver bracelet with clasps gleamed in a barbaric way on her slim golden arm. Temple had not seen the bracelet before. It was obviously a gift from a man.

'Will *mem* and the *dokter* want coffee – later?'

Temple shook her head and hastened from the kitchen to the lounge, her smile for Alan made extra warm by the relief of seeing someone who was friendly and uncomplicated and without secrets in his eyes.

'I take it you've dined at the palace?' she said.

'And how!' Alan stretched his legs expansively across the woven grass carpet. 'Ryk is a true Dutchman and he lays on a good spread.'

'He sent me these drinks so I could be a proper *njonja-rumah*.' Temple glanced round from the drinks table. 'Americans like whisky, don't they?'

'Americans like everything that has a dash of spirit in it.' Once again his smile was meaningful. 'Whisky, lemon and ice, honey.'

'I've no honey,' she said demurely, and mixed him his drink. Her own glass held more lime-juice than anything else, and she avoided the cane lounger in favour of a grass chair as she sat down to enjoy her drink and a chat.

'Here's to good relations between the nations.' He raised his glass and took a satisfying swallow. 'How's work going on the diaries?'

'Without a hitch, so far.' She nursed her glass and studied his fair head against one of her blue silk cushions. In Ryk's company he looked brown-haired. 'I hope your accident case last Sunday was not too bad?'

'I was sorry to have to fly off like that, Temple.' A frown puckered his brows. 'It was an amputation and I hate those things, especially when it happens to a strong and vigorous man. It looked like touch and go for a few days, and that was why I couldn't get back until now. Anyway, I've had a look at Lontah and that boy of hers and they're just fine. She tells me her son is named Dahan Ryk!'

'Yes.' Temple smiled down into her glass. '*Meneer* is an enigmatic man. I thought him quite unfeeling, you know, because he showed not a scrap of pity for my plight. I'd never met a fully adult man before, but I know now that he reserves his compassion for the big things and doesn't waste it on the calf-loves of romantic girls.'

Alan laughed indulgently. 'You look a little different, Temple. Still wide-eyed, but as if your eyes had seen greater things than they had seen before.'

'I feel – privileged.' She gazed across at him, the lamp-light in her hazel eyes. 'You must often feel like that. You save lives and babies all the time.'

'It's my job – may I pour myself another drink?'

'Of course.'

'How about a refill yourself?'

She shook her head, and while he busied himself with the bottles and the ice, she watched the shadow-play of a moth beneath the shade of the lamp. Its buzzing had a low and frantic sound. It could not resist what tormented its frail wings.

Alan stood with his drink and gazed around the lounge. 'You've made this place look very pleasant. New curtains and covers for the cushions, eh? Flowers in the vases, and a few ornaments. It makes all the difference – tell me, is Mei Flower still with you?'

'Yes.' Temple gestured at the plate of biscuits. 'Please help yourself, Alan.'

'Thanks.' He munched a biscuit and cast a glance at the bamboo *chik*. All was quiet beyond it. 'She's certainly unobtrusive.'

'She slips in and out like a shadow.' Temple smiled away the nervousness which always came with the thought of Mei and her mysterious ways. 'Are you staying for the weekend, Alan?'

He nodded. 'All being well. Will you come for that

trip in my flying machine – tomorrow, say?'

'It should be exhilarating – a new experience for me.'

'Do you like new experiences?' He was fiddling with the knobs of the small radio that sometimes behaved itself and let the music flow without too much static to spoil it. It came from a radio-station at Bangpalem, and the late night music was the smooth, romantic kind. A dance tune drifted into the room, an oldie, of which Alan hummed a few bars.

'Takes you back,' he said, 'when you hear music without a group bashing away at a drum-set, strumming on two guitars as though they were banjos, and wailing about the gal they fell in love with at the all-night café.'

Temple laughed, and then it died to a small gasp as Alan whisked her glass out of her hand and pulled her up out of her chair and into his arms. The lounge was fairly large, and being a tropical one it wasn't over-filled with furniture. There was room for a couple to dance.

'It's a shame to waste good music,' Alan murmured.

'I – I'm not much of a dancer – sorry,' as she stumbled over his foot and his arm tightened around her.

'Relax, honey. While you're all tensed up like that, you'll never get into the rhythm of the thing. What's the matter?' He bent his head and laughed against her ear. 'Are you nervous of me?'

'Why should I be nervous?' she fenced.

'We're alone and I have you in my arms. You feel as slim and cool as I knew you would—'

'No, Alan!' She turned her head quickly aside and his lips brushed the side of her neck.

'You're attractive, Temple,' he said huskily. 'I've thought a lot about you during the past week, and I've looked forward to seeing you again.'

'Seeing me, or taking advantage of the fact that I'm relatively alone here?' She tried to twist out of his arms, but his hands were gripping her wrists behind her and her struggles only brought him closer to her. He laughed down at her, a lock of hair across his forehead.

'Did you ever read Swinburne?' he teased. 'He must have had a girl like you in mind when he wrote, "*Smooth-skinned and dark. With bare throat made to bite.*" You can't be a honey-skinned little witch with hazel eyes and not expect men to want – this.' His lips found her throat, and she felt him breathing, and a pain in her wrists from his sudden grip.

She felt all this, but none of the fear, the helplessness that was almost like dying that she had felt on a moon-lit beach . . . in another pair of arms.

'You got hurt, Temple,' breathed Alan. 'We all go through that until we learn not to take life so seriously. Life is meant to be enjoyed, and I see enough of the grim side to know what I'm talking about.'

'What do you mean by enjoyment?' she demanded. 'To me it's swimming with someone, or listening to music, or just walking. It's being companionable, not getting involved in an affair just to blot out the grim side of life. Where does that lead?'

'Do you think that's what I've got in mind, Temple? An affair?'

'I'd be surprised if it wasn't. It's because I'm here, because you think I'm available—'

'That certainly isn't true, you little spitfire.' He laughed and gave her a shake. 'When did you first begin to get the idea that you aren't lovable? Was it at home in England? Or when you got to Lumbaya and found your guy had not played fair?'

'You're a doctor, Alan, not a psycho-analyst!'

'I know enough about the subject to recognize a few symptoms when I see them. You think a man could only want you as a passing fancy, eh? When there's no one else around?'

'I learned long ago that men prefer the ornamental

to the useful,' she rejoined. 'I could always make a good cup of tea, Doctor, even bake a cake – for others to enjoy until they dashed out to a dance or the theatre. I was shy, you see. It wasn't just a case of not being pert or curvy or blonde. I was shy, and no one, until Nick, took the trouble to find out if I could be amusing.'

'Those days are over, Temple.' Alan spoke firmly. 'You've found your feet and, believe me, you don't need to be pert or curvy or blonde to be a girl who gets into a man's thoughts and stays there. Added to which,' he grinned down at her, 'I never did like champagne but always preferred a drink that goes to the heart and not the head.'

He could be very persuasive, she thought, and she gave him a tentative, not quite certain smile. He smiled back at her, and she was disarmed. Alan Kinraid truly liked her for *herself*. He wasn't here saying these things because he felt lonely and had dealt recently with an unsettling accident case.

'You could charm the cuckoo out of a wooden clock,' she said lightly. 'And speaking of clocks—'

'It's time for me to go, eh?' He took her by the shoulders and studied her upraised face. 'Not everyone belongs out in these parts, Temple, but I'm beginning to think that you do—'

'I don't know about that, Alan.' She drew away from him and her lashes veiled her eyes. She walked to the screen door and he followed her out to the veranda. The moon had blossomed since last night and soon it would be full and the feast drums would pound down in the valley. The Dragon King would be propitiated, and the birth of the headman's baby son would be celebrated.

'I never knew that stars could be so big and bright,' she said.

'They smoulder like eyes.' Alan touched her cheek very lightly. 'You have a most attractive slant to your cheekbones, Temple.'

'More therapy, Doctor?' She smiled and leaned against the rail of the latticed veranda. 'Will you be here for the Feast of the Moon?'

'If you would like me to be here for it, and all being well with my scattered flock.'

'What would they do without you?' she said sincerely.

'I make myself useful, but the backbone of these islands are the men like Ryk, and that guy who lost his leg. Without them, Temple, the islands would grow into jungles again. The people who live on them would manage to survive, for there's always the palm tree, the fruits and yams, and fish in the sea. But man was meant to be more than a monkey, let's say.'

'Mijnheer van Helden is certainly able to cope with most situations that arise.' She could not keep a note of restraint out of her voice, for since the morning she and Ryk had walked home together, sharing the gift of fruit between them, he had been cool and aloof towards her. As if he regretted what they had shared that night and morning. As if he shut her out again from his private life and reminded her, by his distant manner, that she was only his secretary and would never be an integral part of his island world.

'You don't find Ryk all that easy to get along with, do you, Temple?' Alan came a step closer to her. 'I'm a little glad about that. He has a certain piratical attraction, which you might have fallen for.'

'You must think me young, Alan!'

'You must know what I think.' He laid his hands one each side of her slim waist. 'Come fly with me, Temple?'

'Tomorrow afternoon.'

'Restrained little English girl!' He bent his head towards her. 'Won't you kiss me, just to be friendly?'

She smiled, then brushed a light kiss across his lean cheek.

'Sweet,' he said, and his eyes dwelt on her lips before he let her go. 'We both have a lot of living to do, and neither of us was meant to do it alone – do you read me?'

'Like a book, Doctor.'

He chuckled as he loped down the veranda steps to the compound. 'I'll see you after lunch tomorrow – I gather you are putting in a morning stint?'

'Like you.'

'What dutiful creatures we are! I have a tooth extraction.'

'Poor Alan!'

'I only hope my hand doesn't shake with the anticipation of our flying date.'

'Poor man with the toothache!'

'Goodnight, *wanita*.' His voice held a wistful note. '*Selamat tidur.*'

'Sleep well yourself, doctor, dentist and counsellor.'

He was laughing as he strolled across the compound to the small gate. He opened it and let himself out, and she returned his wave and watched until the great trees swallowed him up.

She leaned for a few more minutes against the veranda rail and thought how kind he was. She smiled to herself. He was a man who would not wish her to think of that alone. He would hope that his kiss had left an impression; that he had aroused something more than good feeling in her.

She listened to the *kikkers* down in the valley, where they haunted the rice terraces and filled the night with their croaking.

Then she stiffened as she heard distinctly the scrape of something crawling on bent legs up the lattice of the veranda. Her skin crawled as she backed away. She caught at the screen door and hastened into the house, banging the door behind her.

Beneath the beauty of the island at night there lurked

dark things that could frighten you, and hurt you. She gave a shiver and went to the kitchen to make a cup of coffee.

As she lit the stove and set the kettle to boil, she became aware of a pervasive scent. She glanced round and saw a spray of yellow flowers in a china vase. Jessamine, still quite fresh, as if plucked that evening from the palace garden. It grew in profusion just outside the room in which she worked and when dusk fell its scent was heady.

She remembered now that when Mei had entered the kitchen about an hour ago, the jessamine had been arranged in her dark hair. Yellow, scented jessamine from Ryk van Helden's garden.

Temple took her cup of coffee to her bedroom, and it could have been the cause of her restlessness, the half-dream in which she imagined that a scorpion was crawling about in her room.

She awoke suddenly and sat up, feeling hot and finding her bed-covers dishevelled. She reached out to the lamp and her hands shook as she lit it. The light dispelled some of her goblins, and she set about straightening her bedcovers. Instinctively she glanced up at the yards of netting that formed a tent over her bed, and quite distinctly the shape of something dark clung to the pale netting overhead.

She caught her breath and hardly knew how she kept her head and slipped out of the opening so swiftly and carefully. She drew away from the bed, her eyes fixed on the canopy. Yes, there was something attached to the outside of the netting; it clung there darkly, but appeared to be somnolent, unmoving, and was larger than her clenched fist.

What was she to do?

She shrank from the thought of arousing Mei, who

would smile with that veiled insolence that made Temple want to shake her.

Temple felt shaken herself, and angry that she could only stand here like a jelly and feel so ineffectual. *Mijnheer* would calmly shake the thing off the netting, dispatch it, and resume his slumber!

She set her jaw, reached out and gave the netting a shake. Nothing happened, which was not surprising. This time she shook the canopy less timidly, and then jumped backwards with a gasp as the dark object dropped off the canopy on to the mat beside her bed, where it lay unmoving.

Temple couldn't move herself. Several seconds ticked by, and then, a shoe in her hand, she approached the mat cautiously and peered at the object which had scared her.

It was an orchid!

A large, dark purple orchid, with tendrils that curved like legs, and stiff petals that stood out like wings from the striped bud. Seen through the netting it had looked like a large spider ... it had been put there deliberately to give that effect, and Temple had been very effectively frightened by someone who was aware that she was a trifle short-sighted.

Temple forced herself to pick up the orchid – a jungle species which was truly evil-looking – and deposited it in her water jug. She drew a shaky breath, and then tensed again and slewed to face the jalousied door that led out to the veranda.

Something had stirred out there, she was sure of it. She stared at the door, whose jalousies would reveal the fact that her lamp was on, and every nerve in her body was sure that a slim, dark-eyed figure stood out there in the night, smiling behind a veil of silky lashes.

Like the purple orchid, Mei was a creature of the jungle. To some she would appear irresistibly flower-like ... but to Temple she was as sinister as the trick she had played with the orchid.

With nervous decision Temple stepped to the door and threw it open. The moonlight lay bright along the veranda, and beyond it the trees of the compound took strange shapes. The air was alive with moths, and the shrill whistlings and croakings of the creatures of the night.

If someone had stood outside Temple's door, scratching at it with long fingernails to wake her, that someone had now gone silently away and left Temple to wonder if she had been dreaming.

She closed the door with a sigh, and knew that she must ask Ryk to replace Mei ... or find someone else to work on the diaries for him. The orchid in her canopy had been real enough, and Mei might be tempted next time to use something more deadly to frighten her away.

CHAPTER THIRTEEN

THE small aeroplane was lost like a bird in the clouds, and then it broke through them and below lay the glittering ocean and the scattered islands of the Java Sea.

'Which is Bayanura?' she asked Alan. 'No, let me guess! The one that curves like a dragon and is green as jade.'

'What made you think of a dragon?' Alan turned from the controls to give her a lazy smile.

'It's that shape – see the end part that twists like a tail?'

He laughed. 'I'm inclined to wonder if you had a certain person in mind. During lunch at the palace you were rather quiet and pensive – had Ryk said or done something to upset you?'

'No – he wasn't there all morning. I did have something I wanted to ask him, but it can wait.'

'Something important?' His glance sharpened.

'It – seemed important, at the time.' She gnawed her lip, for last night's shadows and alarms seemed unreal here in the bright cockpit of the plane, with so much sunshine below to etch the small fishing boats and their sails against the aqua-green water.

'When I left you last night you were relaxed and, I flatter myself, in a rather happy mood. What happened, Temple?'

'Oh, Mei has a rather tortured sense of fun. She played a trick on me – perhaps I was meant to be amused, but somehow at night, with the sounds of the jungle all around the teahouse, my sense of humour is not at its best.'

'That darned girl! What did she do?'

A glance at Alan showed a hard set to his jaw, and

Temple felt warmed, protected by his concern. 'Put a rather hairy and horrid orchid in the net canopy of my bed. It sounds ridiculous, doesn't it?' Temple forced a laugh. 'But in the lamplight it looked like something else.'

'A jungle spider, eh?'

'Yes. I'm a trifle short-sighted, otherwise I wouldn't have been fooled.'

'I like you in those horn-rims,' Alan smiled. 'They give you the rather grave air of a small girl trying to look like an executive.'

She had been wearing them when he had appeared for lunch at the palace, and that dent of amusement at the edge of his mouth was now explained. 'I wish they made me look stern and not to be teased,' she said.

'Mei will have to go, Temple, or she'll give you a dose of bad nerves. Shall I speak to Ryk for you?'

'No. I'll pluck up the courage.'

'It's going to take courage?' Alan exclaimed with a laugh. 'All you've got to say is that you want another housegirl. Tell him Mei gives you the creeps.'

'It won't be that easy!'

'Why ever not?'

'You men – you can be so blind!' She peered from the window beside her at the waterfalls and gorges far below, and the dense areas of jungle. 'I never realized the island was so wild in parts. I hope you won't run out of fuel!'

'Wouldn't you care to spend a night alone in the jungle with me?' he asked teasingly. 'Or would you feel compromised by a night alone with a man?'

She was about to make a light rejoinder, when her cheeks flamed with sudden colour and she remembered the night she had spent on the steamer with Ryk, clad in his pyjama jacket, into which he had put her after divesting her of her damp clothes. Her blush was not lost on Alan, who was regarding it with a glint of curiosity in his eyes.

'Are you blushing at the thought of being alone with me?' he demanded.

'I'm not that Victorian, nor are you that dangerous,' she retorted.

'Want to put it to the test?' He put the plane into a sudden dive, and Temple held her breath as the jungle green swooped up towards them. They seemed to brush the tops of the giant trees, and a note of anger rang in his laughter.

'Who is he?' he yelled above the roar of the engine. 'This man who's dangerous to be alone with?'

'My one-time fiancé, of course,' she said desperately. 'Who else would it be?'

But before he could answer, the plane seemed to give a nerve-shaking jolt and the next moment it was going crazy in Alan's hands. Now their swoop towards the trees was no longer a game. He was fighting to pull it out of the dive, and yelling at her to put her head down on her folded arms.

She did as she was told, and felt the mad rush of air around the wings of the plane. It was like drowning, and a kaleidoscope of scenes and memories rushed through her mind. The day she had wired Nick at Lumbaya, and had boarded the jet in such an optimistic mood. The day she had fled from Lumbaya and had got on board the steamer in the pose of a boy.

She seemed to feel again the heaving of the deck in the storm, the sound of the waves, the deep voice above her head. . . .

'W – we've cleared the trees,' Alan gasped. 'The beach is just below us. . . .'

The plane shook madly, there was a thud and everything seemed to go dark in front of the cockpit. It was sand whirling upwards and smothering the windows, they tilted at a crazy angle and Temple lurched sideways and felt a fearful pain in her arm. The plane careered to a halt, half buried in the sand of the beach, something ripping at its undercarriage and causing a sudden smell of oil. . . .

'We must get out of here – quickly!' Alan was wrenching at the door beside him, and suddenly the air rushed in, and as he caught at Temple to pull her out she gave a cry of pain.

'I'm sorry, Temple, but I've got to hurt you. . . .' She was pulled free and half dragged, half carried from the wreckage. Then she felt herself thrown face downwards and Alan was lying half over her, shielding her as with a roar the plane burst into flame. A great tongue of it swept close to them, and once again she was forced to stumble across the sands until they were clear of the searing heat.

The next thing Temple was conscious of was that she was propped against the trunk of a tree, and Alan was tearing his shirt into strips and binding them about her left arm. She watched hazily and saw that one strip was tied so tightly above her elbow that her arm was numbed. And there was blood! It was all over her cream-coloured shirt, and the makeshift bandages were bright with it.

'It's a deep cut, Temple,' Alan said tensely. 'It's going to need quite a few stitches and I've got to get you to the hospital—'

'A – are you all right?' she asked shakily.

'I'm darned angry with myself, playing a trick that's landed you with a badly cut arm, and myself with a burned-out plane.'

She gazed over to where the plane still burned and gave off a cloud of oily smoke. 'W – we were lucky to get out alive, Alan.'

'You can say that again!' He stroked the hair back from her forehead. 'How do you feel, honey?'

'A bit sick.' She attempted a wan smile. 'I – I haven't

broken the bone, have I?'

He shook his head. 'It's a deep gash and I've applied a tourniquet to stop the bleeding—'

There he broke off and glanced along the beach to the cliffside steps. Men were hurrying down them. They had heard the crash and seen the smoke and were hurrying to investigate the calamity. Temple fought the faintness that was sweeping over her, and was vaguely aware that Alan had got to his feet and that another male figure was looming out of the mists that were gathering around her jarred and frightened senses.

'I saw the plane go out of control,' a deep voice exclaimed. 'Thank heaven you were able to come down on the beach!'

Then she felt a touch and it was one she would know anywhere.

'Ryk!'

'You could have been killed,' there was a harshness in his voice, and his face just above hers was savage and a little frightening. Temple broke into tears, for at a time like this he might be a little more feeling. He – he didn't have to pounce and look so furious.

'Temple won't be able to walk up the cliffs,' said Alan, in a voice that was sympathetic. 'She's weak from shock and loss of blood. Could a stretcher be improvised?'

'A stretcher is not necessary.' Still he spoke as if he barely controlled an outburst of some sort, but his arms when they lifted her were strong and careful. 'I do not hurt you, *meisje*?'

No, he didn't hurt her. Her arm was quite numb, and she wished the rest of her was equally numb. She let her head rest wearily against his shoulder, and awareness came and went in waves as she was carried up the cliff path. This, she thought hazily, was becoming a habit, and she let her cheek sink against the hard, warm muscles of Ryk's shoulder and the last thing she was aware of was the tang of clove cigarettes clinging to his shirt.

She awoke very slowly, with hardly a murmur, and lay as if lapped by warm and buoyant waves. Slowly the waves turned into the deeps of a mattress, the blueness overhead into the netting of a bed, and sunshine slanted through the window jalousies and lit to a golden warmth the furniture of this large and wonderful room.

A blue and gold room, a great peacock fan outlined against the wall, and a feel of silk beneath Temple's right arm. Her left arm was bandaged from above her elbow to her forearm, and it throbbed when she moved it.

The events of the crash seeped back to her, but what was most amazing was that she should be in bed in this blue and gold room. Only once before had she seen it, but she had not forgotten a detail of it. The blue cover-let – silk in which a concubine was carried to her master. The glitter of the crystal pagoda on the little table be-tween the windows. The Indian rugs against the teak-wood floor, gone from white to a soft ivory.

This was the bride-room which Ryk had prepared for Marta!

The realization made Temple's lips go dry, and she turned her glance to the bedside table and saw that a carafe of water had been placed there, with a tumbler over the top of it. She sat up carefully, wincing as she moved her arm in order to reach for the carafe. She poured half a glass of water and sat sipping it, and her eyes were like those of a startled fawn as she gazed around the room.

The pale jalousies had been fully closed that last time, but now they were partly open and the filtering sun-shine added to the beauty of the room.

So coolly golden, with the touches of brilliant blue to

remind Ryk of the blue eyes that the plane crash in the mountains had closed for always.

Temple couldn't understand why she had been put into Marta's bedroom, and she still felt too fragile to try and fathom the mystery. She lay back against the pillows of the teakwood bed and let herself enjoy the sense of tranquillity which prevailed here. She could hear birds twittering and singing in the garden of the palace, but there was no clock in the room and she could not be sure of the time, or even of the day.

Was it Sunday?

In England the church bells would be ringing, but here on the island only a sense of peace reigned.

She studied her bandaged arm and wondered how she would use the typewriter to do her work on the diaries. The cut must be quite a bad one, for there had been bright splashes of blood all over her shirt. That had been removed and right now she was wearing a pair of silk pyjamas that were several sizes too large for her. She giggled – perhaps she was still light-headed – and wondered what Ryk thought of these constant demands upon his night attire.

The silk was dark and rich, a secret weakness of a man who in most respects was so armoured and self-possessed. And then she remembered the savagery of his expression down on the beach ... the plane crash must have reminded him of that far more tragic one in the jungle hills of Sumatra. It must have brought back some of the pain and terrible choking grief.

Temple closed her eyes ... and in a while she dozed off, as a convalescent will. The opening of the door aroused her from her nap, and she felt a racing of her pulses, an apprehension that changed to a smile when Alan Kinraid strolled into the room.

'Hullo, honey.' He came to her bedside and kissed her cheek in a most unprofessional manner. 'How's my favourite patient?'

'All the better for seeing her favourite doctor.'

'You can say that, after the fool was the cause of hurting you?'

'It was an accident.' Her eyes dwelt on his face as he took hold of her wrist and checked her pulse. 'Will I live?'

'It's racing. Dare I flatter myself that I'm the cause of that?'

'I was asleep and you startled me. Alan, what will happen about your work now the plane is a write-off?'

'Prince Chai will generously provide another. Ryk has been on to him already, by way of the radio-transmitter which keeps him in touch with the prince.' Alan seated himself on the side of her bed. 'Prince Chai would do more than provide another plane to keep Ryk here as his *tuan-besar*. He knows there isn't another manager like him in this whole archipelago.'

Then Alan frowned and glanced down at her wrist, which was still enclosed by his fingers. 'You're jumpy, Temple. Is it reaction from the crash?'

'Yes. How long will my arm take to heal? There's my work, you see—'

'Don't worry about that. Ryk knows you won't be able to use your arm for a week or two.'

'But I want to get the manuscript finished.'

'You mean you want to get away from Bayanura.' He leaned towards her and searched her eyes. 'You spoke about that fiancé of yours while we were flying – Temple, are you planning to go back to him?'

'I've grown up a little since I ran away from Nick.' She heard her own words and realized how true they were. 'I know now what loneliness can do to a person – especially a man.'

'You little self-sacrificing idiot!' Alan looked suddenly angry. 'I won't let you do it. I won't let you throw yourself away on a guy like that—'

'You don't know him—'

'I know his type,' Alan said scornfully. 'They're attracted to the tropical life because they think they can lie about in the sun and have half a dozen houseboys at their beck and call. They drink and go for the local wenches – little men who want to be big men, but who haven't got the backbone for it. Do you see Ryk van Helden stretched out on a long chair half the day, a whisky bottle in one hand, and a dolly in a sarong in his other one?'

She half-smiled and shook her head at the picture. Ryk would never neglect his duties, but like other men he needed to assuage his loneliness at the day's end. When dusk crept over the island and the stars came out. When the jessamine grew scented and heady.

'Not everyone can be as strong-willed as *meneer*,' she said. 'Adversity has made him strong. His work has taken the place of the devotion he would have given to Marta. This was to have been her room. It's very beautiful, isn't it?'

Alan studied Temple in the great bed. 'You look lost,' he said. 'Like a little girl who needs someone to take care of her. Nick won't be up to it – but I would.'

'Alan—'

'I like the way you say my name,' he smiled, and touched her cheek. 'And the way you look cute in male pyjamas.'

As he said this, the door opened and Ryk stood in the doorway. 'I did knock,' he said in a dry tone of voice. 'You were both too lost in your conversation to hear me.'

Temple looked at him and was sure that he had heard Alan's remark. He wore a blue shirt and jungle-cloth trousers, and his eye-patch was dark beneath his mane of fair hair. A big man who had about him a look of unshakable strength ... if he had looked savagely shaken

169

by the crash yesterday, it was because he could never forget Marta and the way he had lost her.

'I have a message from Prince Chai,' he said. 'Another plane will be flown to the island in a day or so. He sends his solicitations, Alan, and hopes you will bear in mind that his honourable pocket is not bottomless.'

Alan gave a laugh. 'Ryk, you could squeeze oil out of a stone!'

Ryk didn't join in the laughter of his friend, but looked rather stern as he towered in the doorway facing the teakwood bed in which Temple was propped against pillows. 'You're looking better, *meisje*.'

'I – I feel a lot better, *meneer*.'

'Good.' He smiled that brief smile of his. 'We want you on your feet in time for the Feast of the Moon. To-night the men will go out hunting for turtles, and the girls will start to prepare their costumes for the dancing. It is our big event on the island – except when a popular marriage takes place.'

Alan glanced at her, and she felt herself drawing back against her pillows. Ryk gave that formal bow of his and was about to withdraw from the room.

'*Meneer—*'

'Yes, *meisje*?'

'I want to thank you for letting me stay – here.'

'Here?' He glanced slowly round the beautiful room. 'It is cool and overlooks the garden, and I thought it would help you to forget the smoke and flames of the crash to have this room.'

She caught an impersonal note in his voice, and was instantly chilled. 'It was kind of you. Thank you.'

He inclined his head, aloof as a stone statue with a pierced eye. The door closed behind him, and a small silence hung between Temple and the doctor.

'You'll give yourself a headache if you try to fathom Ryk,' Alan said with a slight laugh. 'He's one of those who would rather not be thanked for a kindness.'

'When shall I be able to go back to the teahouse?' she asked tersely.

Alan regarded her from beneath puckered brows. 'Don't you like being here? This is the most beautiful room in the palace.'

'I – don't belong here.' Temple looked at the peacock fan and saw a slight quivering of the blue and gold feathers in a draught. 'This is Marta's room.'

'Temple, don't talk like that!'

'It's true, Alan.' She reached suddenly for his hand and clasped its warmth and reassurance. 'When can I get up?'

He glanced down at her hand holding his. 'Your grip feels quite strong,' he said dryly. 'Make it tomorrow after lunch, and in the meantime, honey, stop all this nonsense about ghosts. Marta died a long way from here. She never got to use this room.'

'I know,' Temple said quietly. Alan didn't understand that Marta was here all the same. She haunted Ryk, and this room, and all the places he would have loved showing her. The cliffs and the beach. The secluded parts of the garden where the peacocks wooed each other. The lotus pond, and the stone seat where Temple ate her lunch when she was alone during the day.

This time a tap on the door did not go unheard by them. *'Mari masuk!'* Alan called out. Ranji entered carrying a tray on which stood several covered dishes. He brought *makan* for the *nona,* and a message for the *dokter.*

'From the hospital?' Alan got to his feet.

'Yes, *tuan.* Tea-worker very sick with tum-tum.'

'Ah, that rupture case Khun Lan was worried about! Well, Temple, I'm afraid duty calls.'

She smiled up at him. 'Do you mind being thanked for being kind, Doctor?'

171

'You know I don't.' He spoke meaningly. 'But we'll postpone the event until the Feast of the Moon. I shall enjoy being thanked to the sound of feast drums, and by the light of the pagan moon.'

After he had gone, and Ranji had left her to eat the tasty lunch which the cook had prepared for her, she felt the silence of the room, weighing on her spirit, no longer tranquil.

She forced herself to eat her lunch because she wanted to regain her strength as soon as possible. Ranji brought her some magazines and a book when he came for her tray. He smiled and showed his gold teeth when he saw how well she had eaten. '*Nona* soon much better,' he said happily. 'She eat most of her dinner.'

'It was very good, Ranji.'

He looked at her with an affectionate gleam in his dark eyes. 'Ranji happy that *nona* not die – like other one.'

Her heart missed a beat, and then he had bowed and gone, and she opened a magazine quickly, determined not to give way to that 'ghost nonsense' as Alan had called it. The magazine was an American one and full of advertisements, so she turned to the book. It was a book of poems by Walt Whitman, and she was caught and held by a certain line.

Now voyager, sail forth, to seek and find.

She had sailed and found a strange island, and she had been both happy and sad upon it; both hurt and glad.

Had she meant it, when she had implied that she meant to return to Lumbaya, and to Nick? She tried to recall his face, the last words they had spoken to each other. But they were forgotten, and she knew that Alan was right and that she could not go back to a man she had never truly loved.

She had not fled from love ... she had been seeking it.

Now voyager, sail thou forth, to seek and find.

She closed the book, and her heavy eyes, and there was no sound from the garden. The birds had gone into hiding from the afternoon sun, and even the cicadas rested their restless wings. All was still, all but the beating of Temple's heart and the slight throbbing of her injured arm.

In a while the young nurse, Madu, came up from the hospital to assist Temple with her toilet, and to dress her arm. Madu was honey-skinned and soft-voiced. Her name suited her, and Temple wondered again if this was the girl whom Khun Lan had referred to as more graceful that the bamboo.

'Will you be dancing at the Feast of the Moon?' Temple asked her.

Madu had learned her English from Alan and it held slight American overtones. 'Most Asian girls are pretty good at traditional dancing,' she smiled, 'but I have fallen arches. The hospitals at Bangpalem keep a nurse pretty busy.'

'Do you miss the noise and bustle of city life, Madu?'

Madu ran her hand lingeringly over the silk coverlet she was straightening. 'There is no place like Bayanura,' she said softly. 'This is the palace of the peacocks, and those who leave always have to return.'

And as if to add significance to her words a peacock cried in a hidden part of the palace garden.

CHAPTER FOURTEEN

TEMPLE adjusted the red belt of the linen dress which had been brought from the teahouse. She smoothed the pleated skirt, and caught her own reflection in the mirror on the wall. She still looked rather pale, but she felt much stronger and her arm no longer gave her so much pain when she moved it.

Today she was leaving the palace.

She wanted to go right now, while all was quiet and she was sure that Ryk was down in the valley. She folded his pyjamas neatly and laid them on a chair. She stacked the magazines and placed the book of poems on top. She glanced round the beautiful room and saw that already it had an abandoned look.

A strange air of loneliness pervaded the palace as she made her way along the corridor to the marble staircase. Halfway down she paused and felt a quivering in her legs. It was because she had been hurt and in bed for a few days. The feeling would wear off, and along with it the despondency that caught her by the throat.

She gazed out of the window at the bend of the stairs and saw the tiled pavilions of the palace, open to the golden sun, with their fierce old statues and fountains. Birds lay motionless along the eaves of the high gables, and the shadows of the trees were etched against the tiling.

Suddenly a moving shadow slanted along the tiled courtyard. A pulse beat fast in her throat as a tall figure crossed from among the trees and then paused, as if he sensed that he was observed.

Temple drew back from the window. She stood very still and hoped he would not enter the palace, but even as she gazed down into the hall, he came through one of the archways and saw the glimmer of her white dress upon the stairs.

He came to the foot of the staircase and stood looking up at her. 'Can you manage the rest of the stairs, or shall I come up and carry you down?' he said drily, letting her know in his subtle way that he was aware of her weak legs that wanted to run and yet could not.

She forced herself to walk down towards him, one hand gripping the wrought-iron rail. As she drew near to him, she saw that a certain tiredness was masked by his saturnine smile. 'So you feel you are now fit enough to return to the teahouse, eh?'

'Alan said I could—'

'He is the doctor.' Ryk quizzed her as she stood just above him on the third step. 'I know that you hate to be inactive, but perhaps the palace is too big, too full of echoes, too lonely for you. I have grown used to its size.'

And to being alone, she thought. He did not wish any more for the scamper of young feet across the palace tiles; the laughter of children echoing along the corridors, bringing to life the rooms that brooded behind closed jalousies.

His heart was closed up like those rooms.

'Before you leave, I have something for you. It's a gift from Lontah and her husband, to show their gratitude, and because they feel that you brought luck to them.'

'I – I never expected anything—' She caught at her bottom lip with her teeth, and fought against the weak tears.

'It is the unexpected things that bring the most pleasure. Come.' He placed a hand beneath her uninjured elbow and led her across the hall to his *salon* library and smoking-room. She entered ahead of him and the aroma of clove tobacco awoke several memories that she had tried hard in the last few days to forget.

Exotic, tangy, reminding her of a storm-rocked cabin; of the lusty crying of a baby he had breathed life into; of her cheek crushed to his shoulder as he carried her away from the smoking wreckage of Alan's plane.

'I always thought that girls liked to be given presents.' His voice mocked her, and as she glanced up at him a sudden anger took hold of her.

'What would you know about me and what I like, Mijnheer van Helden? You have never thought of me as a person, only as an efficient adjunct to a typewriter.'

'Hardly, *meisje*,' he laughed at her, and she felt like hitting him. 'At the typewriter you are very capable, but away from it you are like a child for finding trouble.'

'No doubt you'll be thoroughly relieved when I'm off your hands for good,' she threw at him. 'I can't wait for the day to come to get away from you, and your cold palace and its ghost!'

The words hung between them and in the silence a lizard on the wall suddenly snapped its jaws and a gold-winged butterfly was between them, writhing as the lizard began to hammer it against the wall. *Oh, stop!* Temple wanted to cry out. She turned her head away, hating the green lizard and the blue tropics where ruthless things happened.

'You are still feeling the effects of the crash.' Ryk crossed to the lacquered cabinet and opened one of the cupboards. 'Your nerves are all on edge, and this might help to soothe them.'

He handed her a package, which she opened with slightly unsteady hands. She caught her breath at the shimmering brocade which Lontah and her husband had given her. A whole length of it, enough to make a dress, and so supple and silky it slid through her hands like water.

'Lontah thought you might like to make a dress for the feast.' He took one end and draped it around her.

'Saffron – the colour of joy.'

Temple turned quickly to a mirror on the wall and studied the effect of the silk against her pale skin and dark hair. Ryk was reflected tall behind her, but she could read nothing in his face as he took in her thin face and peaked cap of hair, her neck that rose like a bamboo stem from out of the draped silk. 'It's gorgeous,' she said. 'I could never do it justice.'

'Lontah will be disappointed if you don't use it for a dress. She has a sewing-machine and will be only too happy to help you make it.'

'It's more fit for a bride—' Temple broke off and bit her lip, as if to bite back the words, but he didn't laugh.

'Oddly enough,' he said, 'that's exactly the use to which saffron brocade is usually put. Joy and honour are symbolized by it, for honour is a brocade that must not be torn.'

'I hope no one mistakes me for a bride.' Temple spoke lightly as she refolded the silk. 'It's very kind of Lontah to give it to me. I hope Dahan Ryk is still flourishing?'

'Like a young tree.' Ryk looked quizzical as he lit a cigarette and puffed a cloud of spicy smoke. 'Will you have some tea before you go home?'

Home? She thought of the teahouse, brooding among its tamarinds and blossom-trees, and could not think of it in terms of a home. It was to escape the ghost of Marta that she had decided to return, and she wished she could find the nerve to ask Ryk to replace Mei as her housegirl.

'Tea?' Ryk placed a finger beneath her chin and tipped her face towards him. 'No English person ever hesitates over the offer of a cup of tea,' he mocked.

'*Meneer*—'

'Yes, *meisje*?'

But it was then that she caught sight of a trailing mass of jessamine in a vase, and she could not confide to him

177

her fear of Mei. He might jump to the conclusion that she was *jealous*.

'I'm rather thirsty,' she said, pulling away from him. 'May we have it out by the lotus pond?'

Ranji brought tea and almond cakes to them, and she watched the lovely lotus cups floating on their green platters, and thought of the dancing that would take place two nights from now, when the full moon would blaze over the island.

A tremor of excitement ran through her. She would make the saffron brocade dress and enjoy herself at the Feast of the Moon. It would be the only one she would ever attend, and she would make the most of it.

Moonrise. The call of a peacock. Petals closing, and drifting to the ground from the masses of flowers plucked for garlands and for decorating the dark hair of the dancers.

Temple opened her wardrobe to take out the saffron dress which she and Lontah had contrived between them. They had decided to make it simply, with a softly draped skirt and a bodice with a gently scooped neckline.

'I'll wear my moonstones with it,' Temple murmured to herself, and then she gave a broken cry of horror as she uncovered the linen in which the dress was wrapped to keep out the moths. The lovely shimmering gown hung in ribbons. It had been ripped and torn and utterly ruined. Not content with using a knife on it, the vandal had splashed it with a brown liquid.

Temple had gone as white as a sheet, for an odour of coffee emanated from the brown stains. Bottled coffee. The sort which Mei purchased from the village stores.

Temple laid the ruined dress on her bed, and the *chik* curtain clattered behind her as she brushed through it and made for the kitchen. It was empty, and so was the lounge. She turned swiftly and made for Mei's room.

178

She stood outside the *chik* and felt her heart beating fast with anger. 'Mei, are you there?' Her voice shook, and her fingernails dug into the palms of her hands. She wanted to take hold of the girl and shake the truth out of her. . . .

She pushed aside the *chik* and looked into the room. It was empty, and everything was as neat as if the room was never occupied. A pervasive scent lingered, and Temple's hand clenched on the *chik*. It was the scent of jessamine.

She returned to her bedroom and stood for a long moment gazing at the remnants of her brocade dress. She felt cold, though it was a warm and fragrant night, with already the sound of drums and flutes drifting up from the valley. Alan was calling for her any minute, and she searched hurriedly among her small store of dresses for something to wear. The blue one would have to do. She would drape the Indian shawl around it and the red fringes would make it look a little more festive.

Mei must have taken a knife to the saffron dress when Temple had gone down to the hospital that afternoon to have her arm dressed, and Temple could picture vividly the smile on her red mouth as she had ripped open the seams and slashed at the shining silk. Temple shuddered and glanced round nervously.

The teahouse was very quiet . . . a quietness that was intensified by the cicadas outside in the night, and the muffled thud of drums. Temple completed her toilet and hurried out to the veranda, hugging the Indian shawl around her as she awaited Alan.

She was half inclined to go halfway to meet him, but the bushes took crouching attitudes in the moonlight, and she was so unnerved that every little rustle, every slight movement would seem menacing.

At last she glimpsed a white jacket among the trees, and she ran down the veranda steps and across the

179

compound, through the gate and into the arms that opened to receive her.

'*Meisje?*'

She quivered against him, and then drew away. 'I – I thought you were Alan.'

'I am sorry to disappoint you.' His tone became cool, detached. 'He will be delayed at the feast because of an emergency operation on one of the tea workers.'

'Oh yes.' She pulled herself together. 'At the hospital this afternoon he was rather worried about a certain patient.'

'You seem rather shaken.' Suddenly he played the beam of his torch over her face and her dress, and she heard him catch his breath. 'You are not wearing the brocade. May I ask why not?'

She hesitated and glanced back towards the teahouse, with its roofs that curved like horns in the moonlight. '*Meneer*, will you come with me to the teahouse? I – I want to show you something.'

He followed her without question across the compound and up the steps of the veranda, into the teahouse. 'Please wait a moment.' She gave him a quick look, then slipped through the *chik* and a few seconds later returned with the slashed dress.

She showed it to him, silently. 'The dress was like this when I went to put it on,' she said quietly.

'*Het verbast me!*' he exclaimed, and he took hold of the dress and examined it closely. Temple glanced at him again and saw a grim set to his mouth. 'Who would do such a thing?'

'I think it was Mei,' she forced from dry lips.

He looked up quickly. 'Mei?'

'Strange as it may seem, *meneer*,' Temple's voice had begun to shake, 'this isn't the first time Mei has done something to – to upset me—'

'Why have you never told me?' he broke in.

'I told Alan.'

'I see! You confide these things to him – he is more important to you, eh? *Meisje,* why should the girl do things like this to upset you?'

'She dislikes me—'

'Why so?'

'Because she's infatuated with you.' Temple's hand clenched the fringes of the scarlet shawl. 'Infatuation – or love – has an odd way of distorting one's view. She thinks – oh, can't you imagine what she thinks?'

'What do you think?' he demanded. 'That this girl is my – mistress?'

Temple couldn't answer him. The teahouse seemed redolent of jessamine, and suddenly she wanted to get away from it, to the feast and the friendliness, and the dancing that would help her to forget everything for a few hours.

'Let's go,' she said. 'You are the guest of honour, and they will not begin without you.'

She hastened ahead of him out of the teahouse, and soon they were among the trees and the moon was lost, shut out by the vine-laced masses of leaves and branches. The night was filled with wild scents and a strange pagan tenseness. Temple felt Ryk's closeness in the warm scented darkness, broken only by the beam of his torch, wandering ahead of them and fascinating the fireflies, who followed and flickered and added to the mystery of this night of the Dragon King.

They came to the path that led down to the valley, and for a moment they paused side by side to gaze down at the feast fires, and the glow of the festive lanterns. The throb of the drums came stealing up to them, and the pagan quality of the scene made Temple aware of a slight primitive fear.

'Come.' Ryk took her hand and led her down the path. The moonlight struck his hair and turned it to a helmet of steel, and when they neared the foot of the path, the people of the *kampong* came running to greet them and to lead them to the headman's fireside.

The flames leapt and outlined the flowered sarongs, the dark hair in which blossoms were threaded, the ear-pendants and bangles, and laughing eyes.

Lontah was beautifully dressed in a white silk tunic with topaz buttons, an ankle-length skirt of multi-coloured silk, and a new and proudly displayed hairpin of gold and jade. She bowed over her hands in ceremonial greeting, and her husband bade them take the guest of honour mats, which were spread on the ground and scattered with flowers and herbs.

As soon as they were seated the headman clapped his hands and this was the signal for the feast to begin.

Slim girls served the spiced meats, cooked and wrapped in leaves, and handed round great platters of roasted sweet potatoes and pumpkin, rice in oyster shells, and smoked fish. Plates for the guests were of polished palmwood, but the utensils for eating were the fingers, and Temple took her cue from Ryk by rolling morsels of meat in rice and popping them into her mouth. She avoided the spicy sauce-dips after trying one, and caught his smile as he rolled a rice-ball deftly and dunked it liberally in one of the sauces.

Everyone laughed and chatted as they ate, and all at once Lontah addressed a question to Temple. She glanced in appeal at Ryk, who answered for her. Lontah touched Temple's hair and her look was affectionate, and reaching to a great basket of flowers she took out a bloom as big as a peony, with a heart of gold.

She tucked it into Temple's hair, and then resumed her eating with a smile. Temple gave Ryk a faintly puzzled look. 'Lontah asked about the dress, didn't she, *meneer*? What did you tell her?'

His glance flicked the flower in her hair. 'That being

unused to eating with your fingers, you feared to spoil the dress by spilling food upon it.'

'I see.' Temple lowered her glance to the heaped plate in her lap. 'I'm glad you didn't tell her the truth.'

'Tonight we forget reality and enjoy the fantasy of all this. Eat your food, *meisje*. It is very good, *ja*?'

'*Ja*.' She smiled and nibbled a roasted potato, and breathed the smoke and the spice and the heavy scent of flowers. Rice wine was handed round in beakers of polished coconut-shell, and it made her feel slightly heady but more relaxed.

Ryk chatted to the headman, and she glanced round for Alan. There was no sign of him. Nor had she caught a single glimpse of Mei, though instinct warned her that the other girl was here somewhere, concealed in the crowd, watching with dark slanting eyes the man who sat at Temple's side, the firelight in his hair and on the broadness of his shoulders.

Temple wondered what he would say to Mei. Was he shocked that the girl like a flower could display such jealousy and passion? Was he disturbed in any way?

She observed him through her lashes and tried to read his face, but his blind side was turned to her, and he appeared to have little on his mind but enjoyment of the food, the company, and the entertainment.

All this time the musicians had been playing, now all at once the drums began to pound with a new insistence. A pathway had been left clear to the circle of firelight, and all at once men came running along it, their skins burnished and rippling as they lowered the carrying poles on which stood a painted pagoda, almost lifesize, with dragons at its doorway, their eyes glowing with phosphorus red paint.

The men set down the pagoda and retreated, and the twang and clang of barbaric music began to take the place of the drumbeats. No one stirred. Every eye was

183

fixed on the Dragon Pagoda ... suddenly the door swung open and out leapt a glittering, green-clad dancer.

He represented the Dragon King, and wore a fierce mask that made girls in the audience catch their breath with a thrilled terror. Temple must have done the same without realizing it, for Ryk glanced round at her and gave her an amused look. 'This is a dual dance,' he murmured. 'In a while a girl dancer will join him ... she represents the sacrifice to the diety.'

'It's exciting,' she breathed. 'I never dreamed I would ever see anything like this.'

The male dancer had a wonderful flexibility of body and limbs; with intricate head movements he seemed to give the impression of an all-seeing serpent, one who could take all in his path if he were not propitiated.

Girls ran into the ring of firelight and placed baskets of fish and fruit there. They tossed garlands of flowers to the Dragon King, but still he prowled and lunged and looked ready to breathe fire.

Suddenly there was a ching-ching of castanets, a clash of cymbals, and the burnished male figures ran into the ring again, carrying this time the slight figure of a girl. They dropped her to her feet and she stood as still as a statue, her costume shining like water, little stars trembling in the crown she wore, breakable as the stem of a flower.

Temple couldn't take her eyes from the girl dancer ... that grace of a mantis could not belong to anyone but Mei, nor that delicate sway of the body as she began to move her arms and her hands. Long metal fingernails caught the firelight and glittered, and it was as if an Asian idol came suddenly to life.

There wasn't a sound but the sound of the music, and the only movement came from the two dancers, the great musk-gold moon overhead.

A pulse beat so fast in Temple's throat, and the scent of

the flowers was so strong that she felt as if she were choking. Her eyes followed each movement of the lethal fingernails ... she could feel them ripping the saffron brocade, and knew Mei Flower had worn them to destroy the dress.

And now as Mei danced she looked directly at Temple, but no one else seemed aware that it was hate that flashed in her eyes and off the points of her fingernails. They sat entranced by the ballet, and were waiting for the moment when the Dragon was finally overcome by Beauty and let himself be unmasked.

Like idols in a temple they faced each other, while the ching of the castanets and the throbbing of flute and drum grew in intensity – suddenly the glittering fingernails swooped towards the Dragon's mask and tore it off.

Temple caught her breath as the handsome face of Khun Lan was revealed ... agleam with sweat and like a dark golden mask in the firelight. He reached out for Mei, for this was the moment when the girl was overcome in her turn. With the strange movements of a mantis she retreated from him. He advanced and now only the drums were throbbing. He advanced again, and the next moment the slim, quivering mantis figure was caught and held.

This scene took place only a yard or so from where Temple sat with Ryk, and she saw the triumph in Khun Lan's eyes, and then a flash of something else as Mei broke suddenly free of him and whirled to face Temple. She hovered there – mantis-like – and then as if winged she went straight for Temple and the firelight glinted on the cruel metal fingernails. They were poised to stab, to rake, to rip, like the claws of a tigress. ...

As in a nightmare Temple couldn't move to protect herself ... it was Ryk who shielded her with his body as the fingernails flashed downwards and ripped the material of his jacket

In the tumult that followed, Temple escaped and ran off into the night. Like a creature in a dream she found herself down on the shore, alone with the moon, and the whispering sea.

She stood and gazed at the sea of silver, and as tension was slowly drawn out of her, she began to walk along the sands, a slim and lonely figure in a scarlet shawl.

Strange and beautiful Bayanura, where the passions burned with all the fire of the stars. She couldn't hate Mei for what she had tried to do. She could only feel sorry for her, and for Khun Lan, who had thought her more graceful than the bamboo.

The palms and the bamboos waved in a soft, caressing breeze, and Temple paused beneath a palm and rested against the curving trunk. The sound of the sea was so close that she didn't hear anything else ... it was from instinct that she turned suddenly and saw a tall figure approaching her along the sands.

Perhaps it was instinct that had sent her down here to wait for him ... to wait beneath the moon and to find the courage for the encounter.

'How did you know where to find me?' she asked, when he drew near.

'I just knew.' He stood looking down at her. 'Are you all right?'

'Yes.' She watched the sea and the movement of the waves matched the beating of her heart. 'What will you do about Mei?'

'I shall send her away.'

'Poor girl!'

'You can say that after what she would have done to you? She tried to disfigure you!'

'Where is she now?'

'With Alan.'

'Is that why you're here, because he's busy ministering to Mei?'

'He said he would be wasting his time to come.' Hands found her shoulders, quite gently but with a threat in them; a promise to grip and hurt if she tried to run away again. 'He told me that you plan to return to Lumbaya – is it true?'

'Yes – no—'

'What is the truth?'

She looked up at him, and the moonlight was stark across his face and hers. 'Don't torment me – I've stood enough for one night, a – and if I want to go away, I shall go. Why should you care?'

He drew her towards him, deliberately, and all sound but the beating of her heart was mute, distant. She felt his grip on her shoulders and a weakness took hold of her and she swayed forward with closed eyes. Let him be brutal! What did it matter? She was going away, and nothing could hurt any more.

'Do you know what the islanders say?'

'Ryk – please—'

'They say that if a grief pierces no more at the end of three years, then the heart is healed. *Lieve*, if you go away, then it will take three and thirty years for my heart to stop aching.'

'For me?' she whispered. 'Your heart would ache for me?'

'For you, my *liefde*.'

His love ... and love was at the core of her, warming her to an aliveness that was painful. 'I – I thought so many things, but I never dreamed of this. Ryk,' she touched his face, his tousled hair, his shoulders that had shielded her, 'how could I know you loved me when you seemed to hold me off? How could I dare to love you when you seemed to want only what you had lost?'

'When Alan's plane crashed, I relived all the torment, and far more, *meisje*, because you had a reality about you that outshone Marta's dreamlike quality. She would

187

have been something fragile and lovely to treasure ...
but she would never have been a warm and willing
helper; a hand for a woman in labour to cling to; the
crazy nerve to dress as a boy and dare to share a steamer
cabin with a strange Dutchman.

'*Meisje*,' he mocked, 'what would you have done if I
had behaved like the pirate you thought I looked?'

'I – I can't think.' She gave a breathless laugh and
buried her face against him, breathing that beloved tang
of clove tobacco smoke. 'I feel so overwhelmed, Ryk.
Shall I wake up soon and find it's all a dream?'

'Is this a dream, *mijne* heart?' His hands brought her
closer to him and the warmth of his arms was too
exciting, too wonderfully real to be part of a dream. His
lips on hers added to the warmth and the excitement ...
and the promise.

The crushed flower fell from her hair, tossed in the
surf and was carried out to sea, and with it went all the
doubts aroused by Mei and the jessamine she had plucked
from the palace garden and placed in her hair. Her
infatuation for Ryk had never been returned, and so she
had grown to hate Temple. She had sensed, perhaps, that
the English girl would wake him to love again.

Temple sighed happily and rested her head against
Ryk's shoulder as they stood together on the shore of
Bayanura ... the island from which she would not sail
away, but where she would stay to share the delight and
drama with her beloved *tuan besar*.

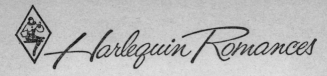

TITLES STILL IN PRINT

TO OUR DEVOTED HARLEQUIN READERS

FOR INFORMATION ON FORTHCOMING NEVER-BEFORE-PUBLISHED
HARLEQUIN ROMANCE TITLES, WRITE TO:

HARLEQUIN ROMANCE BOOKS
DEPARTMENT Z
SIMON & SCHUSTER, INC.
11 WEST 39TH STREET
NEW YORK, N.Y. 10018